HER PATIENT COWBOY
A BUTTERS BROTHERS NOVEL, STEEPLE RIDGE ROMANCE BOOK 5

LIZ ISAACSON

Copyright © 2020 by Elana Johnson, writing as Liz Isaacson

All rights reserved.

No part of this book may be reproduced in any form or by any electronic or mechanical means, including information storage and retrieval systems, without written permission from the author, except for the use of brief quotations in a book review.

ISBN-13: 978-1-63876-140-2

"Sing, O heavens; and be joyful, O earth; and break forth into singing, O mountains: for the Lord hath comforted his people, and will have mercy upon his afflicted."

Isaiah 49:13

CHAPTER ONE

"So you broke up with Farrah?"

Darren bristled at his oldest brother's question. He'd only told his twin, Logan, about the break up, and he should've planned better for Sam's visit to Island Park.

"She broke up with me," Darren said to the dregs of his cereal bowl. Steps sounded behind them, and he hoped when Sam's wife entered, the conversation would be over.

"She broke up with him," Sam said upon Bonnie's arrival.

Darren sucked in a breath and nearly threw his cornflakes at his brother. "Can we not make it a national event?"

"When did that happen?" Bonnie asked, totally ignoring his question. "I thought you guys were happy."

"Apparently only one of us." Darren slid her a glance

but couldn't truly meet her eyes. He'd been existing in this painful without-Farrah state for sixty-four days now.

Sixty-four days since she'd ended their eight-month relationship. Sixty-four days since he'd spoken to her. He'd seen her at church, of course, which was almost enough to convince him to study the gospel at home.

Most of the time, he made it through his morning chores before he remembered he wouldn't be texting the beautiful blonde through his lunch hour.

Rambo, his brother's dog that got left behind when Logan moved to California seven months ago, whined as if he could sense Darren's discomfort. He would never tell his brother, but he'd been letting Rambo into the farmhouse—and onto his bed—at night. The outdoor Australian shepherd loved having his belly rubbed at bedtime, and Darren liked the companionship.

No, he didn't live alone. But Ben lived in town with Rae now, and Sam had moved all the way to Wyoming with Bonnie, and Logan and Layla had gotten married a few months ago and gone across the country to California.

Darren hadn't gone anywhere. Hadn't done much more than saddle horses, and feed horses, and talk to horses.

Shouldn't have tried to get Farrah to do the same, he thought. If he hadn't pushed so hard about her riding in the Island Park Independence Day parade, maybe she wouldn't have called things off between them.

"...you're coming, right, Darren?"

He looked up at Sam's question, having completely missed the conversation for the past several minutes.

"We're doing what?" he asked, not even trying to hide his lack of attention.

"The cemetery," Sam said, giving him an older brother look as he buttered toast and slid it to Bonnie.

She smiled, but her eyes didn't crinkle around the edges, didn't hold the same level of happiness as usual. Darren didn't blame her. She had traveled a thousand miles while six months pregnant. Afraid to fly in her condition, she'd insisted Sam drive them in his pickup truck, and the trip had taken three days.

And they'd come to visit her son's grave. So all in all, the trip couldn't exactly be called a vacation.

"Yeah," Darren said. "I'm coming to the cemetery."

The other two cowboys who'd replaced Logan and Sam came thundering upstairs. Cody and Wade were also brothers, also unmarried, and also not in a relationship. Darren didn't need to feel so isolated, but as the only unattached Buttars brother, he did.

"Morning," Sam said, stepping out of the way so the Caswell brothers could get breakfast.

"Hey," Cody said, grabbing his coffee mug from the dish drainer.

"We're clearing out," Darren said as he stood and danced around his brother to get his dishes into the sink. He followed Bonnie and Sam out to the truck though the cemetery was only about a mile from the farm.

The hay fields that sat between the farm and the cemetery weren't exactly easy to navigate, so Sam went out to the main road and turned north, going back toward town. They drove in silence, and Darren kept his eyes out his window trying to find something about the landscape in Vermont to dislike. He couldn't.

He loved it here; didn't want to leave the way Sam had. Didn't want to start a different career the way Logan had. He loved being a horseman, though the pull of owning his own farm or ranch or boarding stable was appealing. He had enough money from his inheritance to get a decent start, but he didn't want to leave Vermont or Island Park.

So he hadn't even looked—at least until Farrah broke up with him. Then he had seriously considered relocating to a farm of his own. Nothing had caught his eye yet.

Sam parked near Jeffrey's grave, and they all piled out of the truck. Darren hung back, giving Sam and Bonnie their private moment. Bonnie really, who had been married previously, had a child, and then had to bury him after a terrible accident at the park.

Sam kept his arm around Bonnie's shoulders almost protectively, and Darren's heart squeezed at their intimate contact, the easy way they loved each other. Sure, he knew it hadn't always been easy, but everything about them seemed so perfect.

Jealousy lodged in his throat, making it nearly impossible for him to breathe. His lungs kept operating somehow, and he stepped next to Sam and looked down at the grave.

Jeffrey Jones Sherman.

Bonnie bent and ran her fingers along the top of the stone, a sense of sadness in her very movement. Darren took a long drag of air and found a sense of peace in this cemetery he hadn't expected to feel.

He glanced up at the perfectly blue sky, with the wonderfully puffy clouds. The breeze blew across his face, flirted with the brim of his cowboy hat, and he was really glad he was here, in this moment, with his brother.

He wasn't sure how much time passed before he became aware of Sam elbowing him.

"What?" he asked in a voice near a hiss.

Sam jerked his head to the right, and Darren's gaze went that way. Another woman had come to the cemetery that morning, and his heart and lungs and every other internal organ seized.

"Farrah," he whispered. What was she doing here? They'd dated for eight months, and never once had she said anything about anyone dying. Island Park was a bustling town, but he would've heard of a funeral—especially if she was affected.

"Go on," Sam said under his breath. "We'll be a while anyway."

Darren looked at his brother. Found hope in his dark eyes that seemed to be swelling within him too. Sam's lips twitched upward. "Be nice to her."

"*She* broke up with me," Darren reminded him as he stepped around his brother and walked away.

Farrah Irvine had intoxicated him from the moment he'd met her. So what if Logan had set up the meeting? So what that it had been in the lobby of the church? Darren hadn't been able to think straight since last fall, and he actually enjoyed the skiwampus ways his thoughts went when he was with Farrah.

He approached her slowly, his hands way down deep

in his pockets. He didn't want to scare her off. Didn't want to intrude. Didn't want to let her get away.

Her dark caramel-colored hair made his stomach ache. He could feel the ghost of it between his fingers as he kissed her, and the temperature suddenly skyrocketed. With his pulse drumming in his ears, and his breath clogged somewhere in his throat, he stepped next to her.

Said nothing.

Held very still.

She finally turned her head to look at him, but he kept his gaze on the headstone at her feet.

Gary Karl Lewis.

Darren had no idea who that was, but he'd passed away three years ago, just before the brothers had come to Island Park.

"How's Bolt?" Darren asked, his voice barely adding its tone to the symphony of wind. He didn't particularly like her cat, but Farrah adored the gray tabby. Today, though, she stood as straight and still as a statue.

The birthdate on the grave marker was today. So Gary had been born today, July seventeenth, sixty-four years ago. Crazy ideas about how it was sixty-four years ago today that he'd been born, and sixty-four days ago that Farrah had broken up with him started circling Darren's mind.

He'd never been one to believe in fate or signs, but everything in him wanted this reunion to be meant to be. Orchestrated by God. Something other than a chance encounter.

Farrah turned back to the marker without saying

anything about her cat. Darren stood two feet from her, but he felt like an ocean separated them.

"Who is he?" he tried next.

"No one," Farrah said.

Yeah, right. Darren didn't believe her though she spoke in her usual calm way. In all the time he'd known her, he'd never seen her so subdued. She didn't exactly call attention to herself, but she usually wore a quick smile, and engaged in lively conversation, and had candy quirks Darren wanted to explore until he knew them all.

He knew she liked to drink soda with a red licorice straw. He knew she liked to separate her fruit candy by color, mixing the reds and oranges, the greens and yellows, and eating the purples all by themselves. He knew she ate chocolate every day, even if it was just a single square from the stash in her pantry.

"I can probably find out," Darren said.

That finally got a reaction from her. She stepped in front of him, blocking his view of the headstone. He looked right into her eyes, and dang if he wasn't excited to be so close to her after being so far apart for so long.

"Don't do that," she said, an edge in her eye that matched the hard tone of her voice.

"I just want—" He cut off so he wouldn't allow the desperation he felt to color his words. "It's a small town," he finally said. "I'll find out anyway."

She cast another look at the stone and then focused on him again. "Don't," she said again. "If I find out you've searched this out, I'll never speak to you again."

He had no doubt she meant what she said. Farrah

always had. The horseback riding in the parade she said she'd never do proved it. So what if he'd found an old picture of her as Island Park's rodeo queen? Leading the princesses on their horses, that glittery tiara on her head? She said she wouldn't do it—and she hadn't.

Hot, electrical pulses shot through his body when she touched his fingers, then his arm. "Please don't make me do that." Her voice wafted across the inches between them, and he was still trying to figure out what she meant and how to get his muscles to stop twitching from her electrifying touch when she stepped past him and strode away.

After several moments, he got his body back in order long enough to turn around. Farrah had already ate up the distance to her car, and she slid behind the wheel of her sleek, black sedan and put on a pair of oversized sunglasses that only made her more exotic, more like a celebrity.

He couldn't tell if she was looking at him or not, but he lifted his hand in a half-hearted wave, wondering if she'd just said she *wanted* to talk to him again.

CHAPTER TWO

Farrah cursed her luck as she drove back into town. How could she have predicted that Darren Buttars of all people would be at the cemetery on a Wednesday morning? Why in the world was he even there?

Then she'd seen his brother and sister-in-law, and everything had made sense. How she'd told him not to look up Gary also made total sense.

Darren asking about Bolt, her cat which he didn't even like, made no sense.

And the way she'd practically begged him not to do something that would cause her to stop speaking to him made zero sense.

She hadn't spoken to him in two months.

"Doesn't mean you don't want to," she muttered to herself as she turned onto Main Street and aimed her car toward Center.

But she had a line, and Darren had crossed it. More than once. He'd asked her about riding her horse in the parade. She'd said no, citing the fact that she didn't have a horse. He'd gotten someone else to ask her. Tucker. The parade organizer. The rodeo queen.

Honestly, couldn't they find someone else to carry the colors in a parade?

Answer: Yes. Because the parade had happened a few days ago, and someone else had trotted their horse down Center and Main, holding the flag aloft just fine.

Farrah might have been able to handle all the needling, but Darren had gone one step further. He'd actually submitted her application to be the flag-bearer. And that crossed the line, and she had to do *some*thing. It was the principle of the matter.

She missed him though, sometimes more than she cared to admit. More than she'd thought she would. More than she had patience for.

She pulled into the bowling alley parking lot and eased around the building to the back. They didn't open until noon in the summer, and she glanced at the clock as she pulled into her spot. Only ten-thirty.

Didn't matter. She had nowhere else to go and nothing else to do. She entered through the back of the alley, switching on lights as she did. The manager, Guy Mansfield, would be in shortly, so Farrah took a few minutes to go down to the dark, quiet, dead lanes.

When she'd first started at the bowling alley a year ago, being inside such a huge building when it was closed had scared her. Now she only found peace in the way things that were normally very noisy sat quietly, waiting for someone to come enjoy them.

In a lot of ways, Farrah felt the same. She'd lived for several years in the spotlight, with people and sound all around her. But now, she mostly existed on the sidelines, near the back, quietly waiting for someone to come notice her.

She crossed her arms as she stared down the sixty-foot-long lane, the pins down at the end in their perfect formation.

"I like it here," she said to the empty building. The light behind her cast shadows toward the pins, and she startled as the air conditioner kicked on with a hefty clunk of pipe noise.

"Thank you for bringing me home."

She'd fought the Lord every step of the way, but He'd kept at her until she'd admitted defeat and returned to Vermont.

Sometimes, when the bowling alley was operating at maximum capacity, she missed the vibrancy of Los Angeles. Sometimes, when it snowed and she could barely see through the swirling snowflakes, she missed the warmth in California.

But only sometimes, which was a further testament to her that leaving LA had been the right thing to do.

She just never thought she'd find herself back in Island Park, the town she'd vowed never to set foot in again.

"Morning, Farrah," Guy said from behind her and she

turned from the shadowy lanes, leaving her thoughts there for the shiny wood to absorb. They really were very good listeners, and Farrah didn't have to worry about them spreading her gossip around town.

She joined Guy in the snack bar kitchen, where he turned on the ovens while she switched on the fryers. She put pretzels in the oven and opened a giant can of nacho cheese and put it in the hot water bath to warm.

The night crew sanitized the shoes and bowling balls, and a cleaning team came through the alley in the middle of the night. So Farrah and Guy took care of all the food prep in the morning, and a teenage employee would arrive just before noon to rent out the shoes and assign lanes.

"Camry was asking about you," Guy said.

"Oh yeah?"

"She says you're the best babysitter she's ever had." He flashed her a smile before sliding half a dozen mini pizzas into the oven.

"I had fun with her too." Farrah had enjoyed watching the little girl, but she didn't want to make a habit of babysitting for her boss. She'd helped out in a pinch, because it was his anniversary, and Farrah happened to really like his wife Brianna. They'd driven to the city for a Broadway show, and while her jealousy had topped the charts, she'd fed the five-year-old and played board games and watched movies until they both fell asleep.

Broadway wasn't the same as the television career Farrah had been aiming for, but it felt too close to the heart. Maybe that was why she'd been prompted to go to the cemetery this morning though she had no desire to conjure up memories of the man who had abandoned her as a child.

A man she didn't even know existed until a few short years ago. A man whose existence had turned her entire life upside down—literally—and sent her down a path she wasn't proud of. A path she was still trying to come back from.

Just another reason to let Darren find someone else, she told herself as she took the pretzels out of the oven, brushed them with butter, and sprinkled huge chunks of salt on them. But he hadn't gone looking for anyone else. Farrah was connected well enough to the gossip lines in town to know.

Guy's phone rang, and Farrah's pulse pumped out an extra beat. She hated phone calls before the bowling alley opened. It wouldn't be a customer calling; they'd call the alley and the recorded message would tell them when the fun center opened.

No, this was an employee about to call in sick. And Farrah knew what that meant.

"Can you work the front desk while I find someone who can come in?" Guy didn't look weary of his young employees. His fingers flew over the screen as he started texting other people who might be able to cover for the missing teen.

"Sure thing." Farrah flashed him a smile and stepped out of the concessions stand. If she had to choose, she'd rather be in the back, stirring marinara and frying frozen cheese sticks.

But whatever. This was a job she needed, and one she

enjoyed almost all the time. She cast a daggered glance to the only horses in the place—a mural painted on the far wall of the landscape south of town. If she looked carefully enough, she could see Steeple Ridge Farm.

And of course, she'd looked carefully enough while dating Darren, so now her eye flew to the spot with the big brown stable every time she looked at the painting. The stable was only about three inches big in the depiction of the town, but it felt huge to her.

She turned her back on it and used her key to turn on the cash register. She went into the office and opened the safe to retrieve the cash box. With that in place, she checked the shoes, the switches to turn on the lanes, all of it.

The pre-open checklist took several minutes, with the last item on the clipboard to make the rounds of the alley to check for trash, make sure all the racks had the correct number of balls, and pop into the bathrooms to make sure they had been cleaned.

Everything at Pinned was in order, but fifteen minutes remained until they opened. Farrah sighed, realizing that she was ready to go home and her day hadn't even really started yet.

Seeing Darren had really thrown her off her game, and she took a deep breath to try to center herself. But oxygen alone hadn't been enough to help her since she'd broken up with Darren.

THREE HOURS LATER, WITH THE MOMS-AND-CHILDREN CROWD gone, the bowling alley only had one group of older gentlemen still slinging the ball down the lane. The door opened, and a pair of women entered.

Farrah recognized one of them from high school, and her heart shot to the top of her skull. She hated running into old acquaintances, but it was inevitable when she'd returned to her hometown after so many years away.

"Farrah Irvine," the woman said. She wore a bright smile just like she always had in high school.

"Meagan Bybee." Farrah smiled back, though hers didn't feel as natural as Meagan's looked. "What are you doing here in the middle of the day?" She glanced at the other woman, glad she didn't have to be confronted with a pair of old classmates.

Meagan had fared well the past thirteen years. Her skin was still smooth though deeply tanned and she carried a flush in her cheeks. Her copper-colored hair had been pulled back into a ponytail, and her eyes glinted with the color of pine trees.

"This is Audra," she said, indicating the other woman. "We came to meet with Guy about the farm." Meagan scanned Farrah in her jeans and the ugliest bowling shirt on the planet. "I can't believe you work here."

Farrah had heard that at least fifty times in the past year. "It pays the bills," she said, turning to get Guy.

"Whatever happened to your show career?"

Farrah flinched, wondering if it would be too rude to simply walk away as if she hadn't heard. But Meagan was only four feet from her. She'd have to be legally deaf to have not heard. She twisted back, not giving Meagan her full attention.

"Which one?"

"With the horses." Meagan leaned into the counter and turned to Audra. "You should've seen this girl jump. She could make a horse go over anything, no matter what was on the other side, no matter how high."

The way Meagan told it, Farrah had solved the problem of deforestation or global warming. "It was just horse jumping," she said. But everyone in Island Park seemed to remember it differently.

"Always modest." Meagan grinned. "What was your other show career?"

"I tried acting," Farrah said, not wanting to get into it. "Didn't work out, so I came back here."

"To the bowling alley."

Farrah and Meagan had been in 4H together, and the town wasn't that big, so they'd shared a lot of classes too. But they weren't exactly best friends. Farrah wasn't quite sure what to do with Meagan's non-question and look of interest. What was her angle?

"You never struck me as an indoor person," Meagan said.

Audra elbowed her, and the two seemed to have a conversation without saying a word. Meagan really zeroed in on her now. "Didn't you go to college for a little bit?"

"Yes," Farrah said, not quite sure where this line of questioning would lead. She hated with the heat of the sun how much this conversation reminded her of another one she'd had just before leaving LA.

"What did you study?"

"Agribusiness."

Meagan beamed again, practically blinding Farrah with the whiteness of her teeth. "About as far from a bowling alley as you can get."

Farrah finally turned fully, the stitch in her back annoying her almost as much as the redhead still grinning at her like the fool Cheshire Cat. "So what?" She didn't care that she sounded rude.

Meagan's eyes sparked, daring Farrah to get in her face again. "You don't belong in here, Farrah. What if I offered you a job at my family's organic farm?"

Whatever Farrah had been expecting from Meagan, a job offer wasn't it. She blinked, trying to catch up enough to formulate a response.

"We raise tilapia," Audra said. "Year-round. Along with strawberries, ten varieties of lettuce, microgreens, mushrooms, and herbs. It's amazing." She spoke of lettuce as if it were spun from gold.

"Year-round?" Farrah asked. "Even in the middle of the icy Vermont winter?"

"Have you heard of aquaponics?" Meagan didn't wait for her to respond. "We expanded to that five years ago. Audra is a botanist, and she runs our vegetable side. We have an aquaculture guy, and I help bridge the gap between the two."

Farrah had to acknowledge her interest in such a venture. She had heard of aquaponics, and frankly, it would be better than spraying disinfectant in used shoes and handing out pretzels to five-year-olds.

"I didn't finish my degree," she said.

"Doesn't matter," Meagan said. "I remember you from 4H. You had great ideas, and you weren't afraid to try and fail." She glanced at Audra. "She's what we need at the farm."

Farrah's fingers clenched. You weren't afraid to try and fail.

That might have been true once. But now—now Farrah didn't want to fail again. It seemed like everything she tried ended up in disaster, from horse jumping, to college, to acting, to dating.

"Come out to the farm when you finish here," Meagan said. "I'll show you around." She glanced around. "You got a paper and a pen? I'll give you my number."

Numb, and not quite sure how she located the pen and slip of paper, Farrah watched as Meagan wrote Bybee's Botanicals and a phone number on the paper. Then she walked away, her head held high and her laughter floating through the empty building, going into Guy's office and leaving Farrah all alone again.

She stared at the number, at a complete loss for what to do. She recalled Meagan Bybee's family owning an organic farm. A pretty big one too, if she remembered right. Meagan had always been outdoorsy, always interested in how to grow better food for Vermont.

A spark flared to life inside Farrah. She'd once been passionate about things too. Passionate about horse care while competing. Passionate about film and television and acting.

Her fist closed around the paper, crumpling it as the anger she kept thinly veiled rose and broke through her defenses.

She wasn't passionate about anything anymore. She couldn't afford to be.

CHAPTER
THREE

Darren escaped from the lovey-dovey Sam and Bonnie, a crushing load of guilt in his chest. He should be happy for his brother, and he was. Honest, he was. He just couldn't breathe when he was with them for want of what they had.

Or maybe it was the suffocating feelings of abandonment that kept him from taking a true lungful of air.

He'd tried telling himself over the past several months that he was being unreasonable. Intellectually, he knew his brothers hadn't abandoned him. But emotionally and mentally, he hadn't quite arrived at the same conclusion yet.

So he drove north and west from Steeple Ridge, from Island Park, until he found the single-lane road out to the farm where he'd been spending more and more time since Logan had left. He'd come before Logan had left too, but not nearly as often as he did now. The owners let him come in the evenings and check on the plants. Sometimes he helped them harvest firewood they'd use to keep their fish tanks toasty during the long, cold Vermont winters. He always took home something they'd grown, along with their love and acceptance, and a lighter heart.

He didn't dare tell any of his brothers that Jim and Corey Bybee had almost become surrogate parents for him. The brothers had been so united in their grief after their parents had died that Darren felt disloyal needing someone else. But he absolutely needed *someone*. And if that meant he spent his evenings on an organic farm with two people old enough to be his parents, he'd take them.

And they had taken him, too. Just the way he was. Surly sometimes. Quiet always. Sure, Corey asked him questions until he thought he'd explode, but she seemed just as satisfied with one-word answers as she did when he gave her a whole sentence.

Jim sat on the porch most evenings, whittling, something Darren had always wanted to learn to do. He parked in front of the giant farmhouse and grabbed his knife—a birthday gift from Jim last January—from the middle console. If he could just find the right piece of wood, take his chair on the porch, and get his fingers working, maybe he could forget about the encounter with Farrah at the cemetery. Maybe he wouldn't feel so flattened by Sam and Bonnie's wedded and pregnant bliss.

Jim wasn't on the porch, but Darren didn't care. He didn't need an invitation anymore. He could enter their house if he wanted to, open the fridge and find something to eat. Heck, Corey would chastise him if he didn't do that.

He went around to the backyard instead, scanning the ground for a good piece of basswood. Jim grew the trees in clumps, and made marvelous things from them. Dressers, tables, chairs, the mailbox at the end of the lane. Anything he could envision, he could mold out of wood. Today, Darren just wanted something small, and he spotted a long switch of wood that would make a perfect spoon for Bonnie.

Just touching it soothed him, and he settled on the front porch to strip away the bark and start carving the form he wanted. The handle emerged, and he added flowers to it, his fingers working without direction from his mind. He thought of Bonnie, and what she'd like, and the spoon simply presented itself.

He'd just started the bowl when the front door opened and Jim stepped out. Darren had never seen the man wearing anything but a pair of jean overalls and a gray T-shirt, at least when out on the farm. Today was no different.

"Hey, bud." He grinned down at Darren as if he was truly happy to see him. "Didn't think I'd see you for a few days. Aren't your brother and his wife in town?"

"Yep." Darren kept the knife going, the shavings gathering against his cowboy boots. He angled his head down a bit to ensure the brim of his hat hid his face.

"Corey put together a basket for them." Jim sighed as he settled into his chair, but he didn't have a knife this evening.

"Great." Darren didn't want to talk about Sam and Bonnie. Didn't want to talk at all.

"Staying for dinner?"

"If I can."

"Of course you can." Jim got the hint after that, because he didn't say anything else. Soon enough, soft snores came from the chair on the other side of the small table that Corey kept decorated with flowers from the farm. During the winter, one of Jim's ice sculptures became the centerpiece.

Darren slowed his knife and looked up. Across the road stretched fields and trees, all part of the Bybee's land. He'd never felt such peace in all his life. He loved Vermont, especially this little corner of it, and he closed his eyes and offered a prayer of gratitude that God had brought him here.

Even if it had taken a plane crash to kill his parents. Even if it had taken his three brothers leaving him behind. Even if.

He opened his eyes as the sound of a vehicle approached. A few minutes passed before the ritzy, black sedan rounded the bend in the road and kept on coming.

Darren dropped his knife, glad it didn't impale his foot when it hit the porch with a *thud*. He knew that car. Knew the woman wearing the oversized shades behind the wheel.

Couldn't believe Farrah had come out to this farm when she wouldn't come to his.

But sure enough, tall and blonde, so-beautiful-it-hurt, Farrah Irvine unfolded herself from the car and scanned the fields opposite the house before turning and settling her gaze on him.

She gasped when she recognized him sitting there, but Darren couldn't even move. Fury flooded him. What was she doing here? Was she determined to ruin every ounce of solitude and peace he had?

He rose, a roar starting in his mind, but Meagan, the Bybee's daughter, squealed as she came around from the back of the house. "You made it!" The two women hugged, though Farrah didn't exactly look like that was normal for them. "So Audra's got the specs to show you. And you're going to die when you taste dinner."

The word *dinner* haunted him as Meagan led Farrah right past him and into the backyard. She threw him a helpless look over her shoulder, but what was he supposed to do? She'd come out here of her own free will.

And now she was going to stay for dinner?

Darren collapsed back into his chair, dislodging it so it made a loud screech against the porch. Jim startled and yelped as he woke, jumping to his feet and scanning the countryside.

Darren wanted to apologize for waking him, but he couldn't quite get the words out. How was he going to swallow anything with Farrah sitting across the table from him?

"I have to go. My brother—"

"Nonsense," Corey said, sticking a loaf of French bread she'd sliced in half the long way into the oven. "You already told Jim you didn't want to spend the evening with your brother and his wife."

Darren hadn't actually said more than five words to Jim, but apparently his presence on their porch with a length of basswood and his knife had spoken volumes.

Corey speared him with her dark eyes, her chin-length curls springing as she stirred powder into water to make punch. "I was going to ask if you'd come tonight because of Farrah, but I don't need to."

"She's *here*," Darren hissed, his voice coming out more growly than he would've liked. "Does she come out here a lot?" For some reason, that really bothered him. The Bybee's belonged to him. He hadn't had to share them with anyone yet, and he certainly didn't want them falling in love with Farrah the way he had. Then they'd pick her over him, just like everyone else had chosen someone else over Darren.

He swallowed, wondering when he'd allowed himself to become so bitter, so isolated.

"This is the first time." Corey faced him and gave him her full attention. "Honestly, Darren, you two just need to talk it out and get back together."

"Tell her that," he muttered. He removed his cowboy hat and ran his fingers through his hair. "How am I going to eat dinner with her?"

"Audra and Meagan will be here," she said. "And you've seen Meagan. She can't let a moment go by without filling it with sound."

Darren nodded, clenching his jaw and settling his hat back into place on his head. He could use it if he needed to, and he didn't have a whole lot to say most of the time, so his silence wouldn't be viewed as abnormal.

Meagan, the Bybee's only daughter, lived in town with her husband but worked full time on their family farm. Why she'd brought Farrah out to the aquaponics shed was a mystery to everyone. His curiosity combined with his desire to be near Farrah, even if she wasn't talking to him, and he silently took the stack of plates Corey handed him and started setting the table.

The minutes passed and the silverware got laid and napkins folded and before Darren knew it, Jim was banging the metal rod against the triangle to call everyone in from the farm. Dinner was usually a small affair—just family and anyone who happened to be working late. Tonight, there was Jim and Corey, Darren, Audra and Meagan, and Farrah.

No one questioned Darren's presence, and no one paid Farrah a second glance either. No one except Darren anyway.

He couldn't take his eyes off her. She wore a tight pair of jean shorts that frayed along the hem just above her knees. Her blouse didn't seem like something someone would wear to a farm, what with it being white and covered in embroidered pink and blue flowers. But she hadn't gotten a mark on it.

She'd removed her sunglasses from her face, and they sat on her head, holding her loose hair away from her eyes. Eyes that hooked into him with the intensity and power of the blue-green ocean they mirrored.

Farrah met his steady gaze with one of her own, the

same chemistry and attraction that had always existed between them arcing through the dining room as she sat directly across from him while Meagan chattered on and on about how Farrah was going to come work for them.

Even the cheesy lasagna and the toasty garlic bread couldn't tempt Darren's attention away from Farrah. "You're going to come work at a *farm*?" he asked. She wouldn't even step foot on Steeple Ridge property, claiming she was "done with that part of her life," and she "didn't care to be dragged back into it."

Her eyes stormed, but Darren didn't care if his question upset her. He'd wanted her to come horseback riding with him, meet his horse, wander through the woods until they were good and alone, so he could kiss her and whisper how much he loved her without anyone else overhearing.

He never had told her how he felt about her, because she wouldn't come out to the farm. It seemed like everything he loved, she didn't. Everything he was, she despised. Everything he wanted for his life, she had left behind and didn't want again.

"Have you *seen* the aquaponics shed?" She spooned green peas onto her plate without taking her eyes off him.

He had spent hours in the aquaponics shed, which anyone who'd been around longer than a couple of hours would know was lovingly nicknamed the botanical boutique. The way the plants grew without soil was astounding, and he'd marveled at the fish that swam in the partially underground tank.

"You should see it in the winter," he said, the syllables

a bit pointed. His meaning was pretty clear, he thought. *I've been here a lot longer than you, girlfriend.*

She caught the meaning, if the hint of embarrassment flashing in her expression meant anything. He finally looked away long enough to find both Jim and Corey watching him. Corey wore the same expression he suspected Sam would have in this situation.

Be nice to her, floated through his mind. Sam's words from that morning. Corey's silent plea.

"So." He cleared his throat. "What did you like about it?" He knew what she'd say, or at least he hoped he did.

He thought, *the strawberries*, at the same time she vocalized the words.

A smile tugged at the corners of his mouth, and dang if he wasn't surprised when her lips curved up too.

CHAPTER
FOUR

Farrah had always enjoyed eating dinner with Darren. He'd never said a lot, which made what he did choose to utter ultra-important. She'd gotten his message about the farm: *It's mine.*

She supposed he deserved something that was his, though a sting kept pricking her that he hadn't told her about his relationship with the Bybees or about his time out on this beautiful land.

Meagan took over the conversation, talking about two miles a minute about how Farrah was going to come work at the farm the same way Meagan did. "She'll cultivate the new fingerlings, and she's already excited about the third row mushrooms we have growing."

Jim, her father, narrowed his eyes and chewed. He swallowed and said, "Why do we need another person doing what you're doing?"

Meagan's whole face turned red, and she suddenly didn't have anything to say. Farrah hadn't realized she'd be taking over for Meagan. She shifted uncomfortably as she waited for Meagan to say something.

She had loved the two hours she'd spent in the aquaponics shed. She loved the symbiotic relationship between fish and plant. She'd heard of soilless growing, but she'd never seen it. And all those strawberry plants growing in water had taken her breath away. For the first time in years, she felt like she was where she was supposed to be.

That comfortable feeling evaporated as Corey said, "Meagan?"

"Luke and I are expecting." Meagan's smile grew and grew until Farrah thought it would crack her face.

Corey squealed and leapt from the table, nearly sending a plate full of butter into Darren's lap. Audra gasped and then started laughing. "That's why I had to wait for twenty minutes in your driveway today while you were 'getting ready.'"

"I was sick," Meagan insisted, standing to accept her mother's hug.

Farrah felt like an intruder on this private family moment, but she supposed there were as many non-Bybees present as there were Bybees. Darren smiled, but he continued eating while the hugging and exclamations continued. While Corey asked Meagan when she was due. While Audra gushed about the baby shower she'd throw.

A writhing feeling started down in Farrah's stomach. A

writhing that spoke of lost opportunities and a life without children. Just another reason to find something she could fill her life with. Something she could feel fulfilled doing.

And she knew it wasn't at Pinned, but right here at Bybee's Botanicals.

"So I'll train Farrah to do everything I do, so when the baby comes, the farm will carry on as normal." Meagan spoke like she made the decisions for the farm. Maybe she did.

"So it's just you and Audra that run the aquaponics shed?" Farrah asked.

"Darren volunteers," Jim said.

Farrah whipped her head to him, noticing out of the corner of her eye that Darren did too. Oh, and the choking coming from his mouth was a dead giveaway that he was surprised to hear he volunteered in the aquaponics shed.

"Darren does all kinds of things around the farm," Corey said.

He volleyed his gaze to her, but Farrah watched Meagan, who didn't seem surprised or worried about what her parents had said.

"Yeah, Darren sometimes chops wood from the farm to keep the tilapia ponds the right temperature in the winter. He's sapped trees. Cleared a road once. And he likes to hang out near the strawberries, same as you." She grinned that mega-watt smile Farrah had been jealous of earlier.

"He likes his dipped in chocolate," Farrah said, not quite sure when the words had entered her mind or why she'd decided to speak them.

Darren's gaze flew to her now, and she almost laughed at the poor, whiplashed look of him.

"*White* chocolate," Corey amended. "With graham cracker crumbs on top of that."

"Like a shortcake," Meagan said, glancing around the table for confirmation.

Farrah leaned back in her chair and folded her arms as an agonized look paraded across Darren's face. She knew what he was thinking: *Stop talking about me.*

"So is the aquaponics job full time?" she asked, giving him what he wanted most. She knew, because obscurity in a crowd was what she craved too. And yet, somehow, they'd found each other.

"Definitely," Meagan said. "And then some."

Corey sat back down and nudged the lasagna pan closer to Darren, who took another piece and kept eating. "We'd love to have you, Farrah. Meagan mentioned something about an agribusiness degree?"

Farrah shot a sharp look at Meagan. "Not a degree. I went to two years of college. I'd barely started in the agribusiness…business."

"She's a thinker," Meagan said. "I'm telling you, she'll triple our vegetation production, and she's already mentioned bringing in trout during the colder winter months."

"Trout take twice as long to rear," Jim said. "We can do two tilapia harvests in the time it takes to raise one batch of trout."

"I know, Dad," Meagan said like they'd had this discussion before. "The point is, she thinks. She doesn't just look at what we're already doing and go, 'Oh, okay. Sure, just let me show up and keep this lettuce alive.'"

Well, that *was* sort of how Farrah had been thinking. Actually, she'd been so overwhelmed with the sheer size of the shed, the number of plants growing, and the wonder of the system that she hadn't given much thought to anything else.

Fine, Darren. She'd thought a lot about Darren.

Seeing him sitting on the porch like he belonged there had sent a heated shock right through her. She hadn't been able to tell what he'd been doing, and Meagan had whisked her away so quickly she hadn't been able to say a word to him.

She found herself wanting to be alone with him, just for a few minutes. Just to explain that she wasn't here to take anything from him. Wasn't here to torture him.

The conversation continued, and Farrah fell silent. Darren finished eating long before everyone else, but he had an easy way of being so no one seemed to notice that he was done when they weren't.

Farrah had always marveled at his physical strength. His stamina for working long hours on a horse farm. She knew what that took, and it wasn't easy. She hadn't been quite as prepared for his spiritual power, or that he was simply a nice guy. In her experience, a man never came with the whole package. Concessions always had to be made.

But it seemed like Darren Buttars had broken that mold. No, he didn't talk much. He was pushy. And sometimes impatient, especially when he didn't understand the reasons for something. But simply sitting around a dinner table with him was easy, casual, fun.

Everything Farrah wanted in her life.

She questioned herself for the tenth time that day. Questioned why she'd broken up with him and cut off all contact.

He stood first, long before usual if the panicked look on Corey's face was any indication. "I should go."

"Let me get you a plate for tomorrow."

"It's—" He watched Corey rush into the kitchen before he could protest. Fondness entered his eyes, and Farrah's chest clenched tight. He'd confessed to her that he really missed his parents, and it was obvious he viewed Jim and Corey Bybee as the mother and father figures he didn't have in his life.

"I'll get that basket for Sam and Bonnie." Jim tossed down his napkin and stood, ambling off in the same direction his wife had gone.

Audra whispered something to Meagan and the two of them stood. Farrah caught the words, "…not my boyfriend," from Audra, but the blush riding in her cheeks indicated that whoever she and Meagan were talking about was definitely more than just a friend.

Farrah inhaled, and she was alone with Darren. He gripped the back of his chair with both hands and kept his head down. She couldn't see his handsome face through his cowboy hat.

"How long have you been coming out to the Bybee's farm?" she asked.

"A while," he said.

"While we were dating?"

He lifted his eyes to hers, and she sucked in a breath at the beauty of him. "Yes."

Farrah nodded while a knotted weight settled behind her lungs. She hated this feeling, and it wasn't fair to blame him for finding a place of safety, a place to have the relationship he craved. It wasn't his fault she hadn't told him about her family.

"Are you really going to work here?" he asked.

Farrah nodded, employing his method of saying less.

"You do realize they have a whole stable full of horses, right?"

She couldn't tell if he was trying to make her mad, just letting her know, or something else entirely. Darren held everything so close, shuttered off behind closed doors, and she'd had to get him alone, hold his hand, and smile at him before he'd open up. Once she got him talking, though, the man could spill a lot of secrets.

Farrah missed the sound of his voice. Missed the tenderness in his touch. Missed the warmth of his embrace, and the taste of his mouth.

She held him behind such a tall wall, and it was exhausting.

"How many horses?" she asked.

Darren blinked and chuckled. "Guess you'll find out." He turned his back on her and walked into the kitchen. She heard the low murmurs of his voice mingling with the Bybees, and she couldn't bear to stay in the dining room alone.

She slipped out the front of the house, wondering

where everyone else had parked. The chair where Darren had been sitting when she arrived looked inconspicuous now, but she examined it. A few fine shavings of wood dusted the ground, and she wondered if he'd been carving.

She hadn't even known he knew how to carve wood. Her emotions tangled until she couldn't separate them to identify them, and she practically leapt down the stairs in her need to get away from this farm.

"Two weeks notice?" Guy frowned like he didn't understand the words. "You're quitting?"

Farrah tried to smile, but it came off wrong. "I found another job."

Guy sighed and pulled out a package of frozen pretzels. "You're the best manager I've had."

She wasn't sure if she should feel proud of that or not. And she really wanted something in her life she could be proud of. "A great opportunity came up with this aquaponics farm."

"Aqua-what?" Guy arranged four pretzels on a tray and slid it into the oven.

"It's soilless farming," she said. "I went to two years of college in agribusiness, and this is something that actually interests me." She realized how that sounded as the words left her mouth. "I mean, this is great and all, and I've been so grateful to have this job, but—"

Guy waved her into silence. "I understand, Farrah. He

moved toward the exit of the concessions kitchen. "I'll get the word out that I need someone during the day."

"I'll help train whoever you get," she called after him, adding, "Sorry, Guy," in a much softer voice he couldn't hear. But she couldn't make her life decisions based on how someone else would feel. Not again.

So she worked her hours at the bowling alley, and she went out to the farm after that. She learned to park her car past the house, down the road around the bend, and next to the aquaponics shed. She'd learned about the ten varieties of lettuce the Bybees grew. She read articles on raising tilapia at night. She dreamed of monitoring water temperatures and segregating the huge, twenty-thousand gallon fish tank into the warmer climate the tilapia needed and the cooler water temps that trout would like.

She never saw Darren again, but she recognized the old truck she'd ridden in more times than she could count. She'd kissed him in that truck, and when she pulled into the farm after finishing her last day at the bowling alley, that truck taunted her with memories she wished weren't quite so close to the surface. Or maybe she kept them there, the way her weaker tilapia lingered near the surface, so she could relive them at a moment's notice.

She hadn't once seen Darren in the botanical boutique, as she'd learned everyone called the aquaponics portion of the farm, but as she pushed her way into the greenhouse, she found him on a ladder, fixing a panel on the far end of the shed.

Her heart lurched and started tap dancing in her chest.

Annoyance that the simple sight of him made her react like she could still kiss him if she wanted to.

No, she realized as she wandered down the aisle toward the mushrooms she'd been tending, her nerves and body reacted the way it did because they were *anticipating* kissing him again.

CHAPTER FIVE

Darren worked to finish the repairs in the shed, very aware that Farrah had arrived an hour ago. He'd tried to get off the farm before she showed up, as he'd managed to determine her arrival time at five-fifteen each evening. She obviously came straight out to the farm after her shift at the bowling alley. But tonight, Meagan had asked him to fix a few broken panels in the greenhouse from last night's windstorm.

He couldn't say no to her, and he'd been circling an idea for the past two weeks. Circling Farrah so their paths didn't cross. Always circling.

Sam and Bonnie had gone back to Wyoming, and though Ben lived in town with Rae, they hadn't come out to Steeple Ridge for Sunday dinner like they usually did, citing that Rae was ill. Which was just fine, because neither Darren, Cody, nor Wade could cook much more than a grilled cheese sandwich.

Missy usually brought food, and Rae and Ben usually came, and Darren usually made it through the week by living on the promise that he wouldn't be alone on the Sabbath. But none of that had happened, which had left Darren feeling vulnerable and irritable at the same time.

So he'd kept his eyes on his work though Farrah's scent teased him as it got caught up in the air filtration systems and reached him from his position atop the ladder.

By the time he'd replaced the glass and put the ladder away, he didn't have any willpower left. If he ran into Farrah, he wasn't sure what he would do. So all he could do was pray she'd already left.

He stepped out of the massive botanical boutique, practically running over her as she tried to enter. He grunted and reached out to steady her. Somehow, though, his arm swept around her and held her against his body, the way he'd done dozens of times before.

She righted herself and he steadied, a zing of attraction and desire cascading through him. "Sorry," he muttered as he released her and stepped back. He dipped his chin to his chest and moved to the side to let her in.

"You're not staying for dinner?" she asked.

"Are you?"

"Corey is a good cook."

Darren looked up, betrayal filling his chest. He hadn't been staying for dinner, because he left before it was time to eat. Again, because of Farrah. He'd already lost so much because of her, and a fire entered his bloodstream he hadn't felt in a while.

"As good as you?" he asked.

Farrah shrugged, her humility ever-present. It was one of the things Darren had first loved about her. He wanted to taste her pork chops with onion gravy right now; the creamy mashed potatoes she made tasted more like butter than anything else.

"Yeah, I think I'll stay for dinner." He took a step closer, his mind swirling around that idea he'd had. "Maybe you'd teach me how to cook, and I'd be able to take care of myself."

His words had the desired effect as Farrah's face flushed and she drew in a quick breath. When they were dating, she'd often joked that she needed to give him a few cooking lessons so he'd be able to survive on his own. Darren had always assumed she'd teach him after they were married, or she'd simply tease him about his lack of culinary skills for the rest of their life together.

He wasn't really asking her for a cooking lesson, and they both knew it. He was asking her out. Right there, right now.

She couldn't seem to look away from him. Those teal eyes held him fast, and he reached for her. "Farrah," he said, her name like poisoned honey on his tongue. He brushed his fingers against hers and wanted to grab on and never let go.

"I just want…. Can we just talk?" He had a whole lot more to say, but the words seemed stuck behind a dam in his throat.

A flash of a smile touched her lips for a moment. "I'd— I want—"

The clanging of the dinner triangle interrupted her. She

turned back toward the house, just across the field. "I'm starving." She turned and walked away from him, her hips swinging with every step.

Darren watched her go, wondering what, exactly, she was hungry for. Because he was starving too, but it wasn't for want of food.

The next day Darren had just brushed down Paintbrush after working him in the fields when Cody came into the back barn. "There's a Jim Bybee on the phone, and he says he needs you out at the farm." Concern crossed the other cowboy's face. "I told him you were already out on the farm, and he said Alaska's loose, and then he hung up."

Darren didn't hesitate. He reached for his rope hanging on the wall and started for the door. "Alaska's his horse," he said. "And Jim Bybee owns the organic farm north of town." He hustled outside into the bright sunshine, already late and wishing he hadn't had to wait for the message about Alaska.

He made it to the farm in under fifteen minutes and skidded to a stop next to the stables on the opposite side of the farm from the aquaponics shed. Corey stood there, wringing her hands. "Jim left Slate for you," she said. "Alaska unlatched the west gate and got out. Jim's been out for an hour trying to find her."

Darren glanced at the shiny black sedan parked in the wrong place. He didn't have much time to comprehend why Farrah had parked all the way over here when her work was in the building on the other side of the farm.

He swung onto the slate gray horse that had been saddled for him and pressed his hat further onto his head. "West?"

"Well, I'm—we're not really sure."

Darren gripped his rope and headed out on the horse, his eyes scanning the fields, the horizon, the tree line for any movement, any flash of white against the green. Alaska was a stubborn old horse—Jim's favorite, of course—who had a soul that couldn't be contained behind a fence.

Worry wormed its way under Darren's skin. Jim would be devastated if he lost Alaska. The steady rhythm of hooves lifted into the sky as Darren worked his way along the line between the house and the outbuildings and the pastures.

Another rider appeared from out of the trees, and Darren lifted his hand to Jim. He pointed farther north, and Darren swung his horse that way. Only a moment later, another rider appeared, this time on a bright brown horse named Featherwing.

It wasn't hard to see the feminine figure despite the distance between them. The woman wore a hat, but her blonde curls cascaded over her shoulders and down her back.

It was Farrah.

Riding a horse.

Wearing a cowgirl hat.

And boots.

Darren almost slid right off Slate's back, and his mouth practically hit the dirt. She turned and joined Jim as they moved north, leaving Darren there in a state of shock. Once that wore off, all that remained was anger. She'd sworn to him that she'd never ride again. She'd resisted every request of his to come to Steeple Ridge. She'd broken up with him over riding a horse and carrying the colors in a small-town parade.

He almost turned Slate right around and went on back to the farm he knew. The farm where he'd never have to see Farrah and experience such a tidal wave of fury.

Why could she come here and ride these horses and she couldn't come to his farm and ride his horse?

The need to leave shot through him with the force of lightning. But he couldn't do that to Jim. So he made his horse follow theirs. He'd nearly urged Slate to pick up his trot when a noise from the trees to his left caught his attention. A flash of white cut through the shady darkness under the limbs, and Darren swung his horse that way.

"C'mon, Alaska," he called, approaching slowly. The horse huffed, shuffled in the undergrowth. Darren's fingers tensed around the rope and he released the loop and let it hang.

"You gotta come on back to the corral." He paused Slate as Alaska came into full view. The horse had a wild look in her eyes, and her coat was slick with sweat. She had to be tired and thirsty and Darren thought he could get her back without the rope.

Her eyes twitched to his right, and Farrah appeared on her horse. Darren warned her off with a lifted hand, and she stilled. He drank in the sight of her on that horse, and everything in him ran a little hotter. And he hated that, because she'd made her position about their relationship really clear.

She'd walked away last night. Hadn't said a single word to him during dinner. Darren felt like his heart was being broken all over again, and he wondered how many more cracks he could sustain before the thing would stop beating altogether.

"C'mon," he said to the horse. He needed to turn away from the sight of Farrah on that horse, and he hoped Alaska would simply come with him. Slate had taken four steps when Darren heard Alaska begin walking too.

She fell into place on Slate's left flank, and Darren led her back to the corral without throwing his rope at all. Corey dialed her phone as soon as she saw them, and Jim arrived just as Darren closed the gate behind them, Alaska properly contained.

Darren swung off Slate and flipped the reins over the top rung of the fence. He turned his attention to Alaska and started brushing her down, the horse's eyes falling halfway closed. He wanted to lecture her, pour out his frustration with Farrah to her, but he let the words come out silently in in every brush stroke.

With her properly cared for, he let Slate into the stable too. Farrah stood a couple of stalls down, her hands stroking Featherwing's neck. Darren scoffed and turned away. He couldn't even speak to her right now, and he didn't turn back when she called after him.

As he jumped back into his truck and got out of there,

he thought maybe he finally understood how Farrah had felt, why she hadn't been able to talk to him, after he'd submitted her name for the flag bearer in the parade.

He slammed on the brakes and threw the truck in park. He marched back down the street and right back into the stable. "I'm sorry, okay?" His voice echoed through the building, startling even himself. Farrah turned toward him, her cowgirl hat bathing her face in shadows.

"I said it a dozen times back in May, and I still mean it. I'm sorry I pushed you to ride in the parade." But she should see herself atop a horse. She was beautiful and magnificent and it was clear she belonged in the saddle. Why couldn't she see that? Why didn't she want it?

Farrah took a step toward him, but he backed up to keep the distance between them.

"I hated seeing you on that horse," he said, bitterness in every syllable. "Why—How—Why can you ride here and you won't come to Steeple Ridge?" Pure agony carried in his question, amplified with every second that passed. And passed. And passed.

Unbelievable. She still wasn't going to talk to him, really tell him what was going on with her. Darren ground his teeth together, willing her to say something. *Any*thing.

He finally shook his head. "Whatever, Farrah." He stepped to the door and practically ripped it off its hinges. "*I* don't want to talk to *you* anymore." His statement couldn't be further from the truth, but he couldn't keep opening his heart to this woman only to get it sliced and diced into bite-sized pieces.

He hated this cycle he and Farrah seemed to be in. This

anger was only the first step. Then he'd withdraw for days, maybe even weeks. During that separation, he'd soften and forgive her, and then he'd try to get close to her again. Then she'd say or do something—or *not* say or not do something he wished she would—and his frustration would get the better of him and he'd walk away from her again.

"Time for a clean break," he told himself as he reached his truck and fired up the engine. Totally clean.

If only he could figure out how to purge Farrah and all the memories they'd shared as easily as he could drive away from the stable where she still hid.

CHAPTER **SIX**

I don't want to talk to you anymore.

Darren's words lashed her insides with hot tar. Just as quickly as that pain came, more of what he'd said made her muscles cramp.

I hated seeing you on that horse.

Her body hadn't particularly liked it either. Holding herself upright in the saddle required muscles she hadn't used in a long time. But Jim and Corey had wormed their way into a soft spot in her heart, and when his prized horse had gotten out, Farrah hadn't even hesitated.

It was nice to know that saddling and swinging onto a horse was like riding a bike. Though she hadn't done it for a dozen years, she still knew how. Her fingers still knew exactly what to do.

She finally managed to move her feet enough to get her out of the stable. Darren was long gone. So were Jim and Corey. Farrah felt the same way she had those twelve years ago when she walked away from Steeple Ridge, vowing never to return.

Deflated. Defeated. Depleted.

Darren wanted to ride with her so badly, share his farm life with her so much, and she'd denied him that. She hadn't understood until ten minutes ago, with his handsome face contorted with pure agony, his questions lifting into the rafters, how much she'd hurt him by refusing to go out to Steeple Ridge.

But how could she explain to him what had happened there? She didn't talk about it with anyone—she never had. She'd bottled everything up and left Island Park for college in another state.

She slid into her car, her muscles tight tight tight, and her mind whirling. So she'd need to adjust to horseback riding again. She'd realized after only a moment in the saddle how natural it felt. How much more like herself she felt. How big of a piece of herself she'd thrown away all those years ago.

"Who cares that Paul Fletcher wasn't your real father?" she asked herself as she started the ignition. She sat in the idling car, contemplating where she should go. To Burlington, where her mom and dad lived? But not her biological parents. The thought still brought a pinprick of breathlessness to her lungs.

To Steeple Ridge, where the only man who'd ever made her feel loved was probably storming around, saddling his own horse so he could escape into the forests beyond the farm and try to forget the argument he'd just had with her?

She backed away from the stable and set the car down

the dirt lane back to the highway. Farrah usually smiled as she passed the Bybee's Botanical Farm sign, with the slogan "From Scales to Strawberries" along the bottom.

But today, the words she'd fallen in love with blurred as her eyes filled with tears. When she got to the highway, she didn't turn north toward Burlington. She'd been back in Island Park for over a year, and she'd gone to see her parents once. They'd come to Island Park to board their horses at Steeple Ridge once, and they'd met her for lunch afterward.

That was all she'd been able to do. She thought about them every day, and with each passing hour, she knew she'd be able to forgive them one day soon. She glanced in the rearview mirror, but nothing prompted her to turn around.

She swung into the grocery store parking lot and kept her sunglasses on all the way into the produce section. Only then did she push them up to examine onions, microgreens, and garlic cloves. She shopped slowly, deliberately, going through her mental grocery list dozens of times to ensure she didn't miss a single ingredient.

On a whim, she tossed a package of marshmallows, a box of graham crackers, and a super-sized bar of chocolate in the cart. She wasn't sure if the farmhouse at Steeple Ridge still boasted the large fire pit she'd sat around as a teenager, but if it did, she wanted to be armed with s'mores ingredients.

The fact that a perfectly toasted s'more was one of Darren's favorite treats didn't have anything to do with her decision. She sighed as she recognized the internal lie.

Darren seemed to influence every decision she made, whether he knew it or not. Whether she consciously acknowledged him in her decision-making process or not.

But as she'd been researching the agribusiness degree at the University of Vermont this past week, Darren waited right there in her mind. The university was in Burlington; she'd only have a half an hour's commute. Maybe Darren would be able to help around the botanical boutique in her absence.

And if she taught him to cook, maybe he'd have dinner on the table when she got home from classes.

The fact that she was thinking of him as if they were married was absolutely ridiculous. He had a full-time job at another farm and could barely boil water. She lived in a small house in an older section of town, with dozens of bushes and flowers she enjoyed cultivating through the spring and summer months. With the exception of the past few weeks where she'd been eating with the Bybees, Farrah made dinner every evening. Cooking relaxed her, brought her closer to her center, helped her know her true self.

She hoped it would do so tonight, but the way her stomach turned and her heart jumped in her chest, she suspected it wouldn't.

She pulled out her phone and sent a text. I'm coming out to do your first cooking lesson. Does four-thirty work?

He didn't answer while she loaded her groceries onto the belt and paid. He didn't answer on her drive home, or as she took the groceries into her house. Four o'clock came, and he still hadn't answered.

Maybe he'd done exactly as she'd predicted and saddled his horse for a long ride through the forest, where he didn't have cell service.

Maybe he'd meant it when he'd said he didn't want to talk to her anymore.

Maybe his agony had finally been too much to overcome, and she'd never see him again.

The thought hurt too much to think about for more than a few seconds, and Farrah pushed it out of her mind. She loaded up what she needed to make his favorite meal, put it in the backseat of her sedan, and got behind the wheel.

She thanked the Lord for air conditioning as the minutes ticked by and she still couldn't get herself to put the car in drive.

If she didn't leave now, she'd be late.

But did it really matter? Darren hadn't confirmed that she could even come out to the farm at four-thirty.

Just go, she told herself. But she couldn't. So she switched her plea toward heaven. *Please help me to go out to Steeple Ridge.*

For a while in California, Farrah had slept through church on Sunday mornings. Done things she'd never done before. Spoke about being married. Being away from the presence of God had alerted her to just how much she craved His influence.

Now, she was able to put the car in reverse and get herself on the road. By some miracle, she navigated to Steeple Ridge Farm with ease, seemingly in the blink of an eye. She knew which road to take to go to the farmhouse instead of the general public parking lot.

As she turned onto the road before the curve that led around the farm, she gripped the steering wheel as memories assaulted her from every side.

She'd performed in dozens of horse shows out at this farm. She'd had her first kiss with a junior champion around the corner of the main barn while her dad loaded up her horse. She'd fixed fences for Jamie Gill, the woman who used to own the farm before she'd retired a few years ago. She'd spent as much time at Steeple Ridge as she did at school, and both of those more than she had at home.

She pulled into the dirt driveway behind Darren's truck, wondering if that was a smart move. He didn't like feeling trapped, something Farrah understood better than most.

A man stepped out of the farmhouse, but it wasn't Darren. Another cowboy who wore jeans and a red shirt along with a black cowboy hat. Darren always wore a charcoal-colored one, the exact shade Farrah preferred on men.

This guy leaned against the pillar on the porch and tipped his hat at her. A golden retriever emerged from the house and sat at his feet.

With nothing else to do, Farrah got out and lifted her hand in a wave. "Is Darren here?"

"Out in the fields," the man said. "He left his phone on the kitchen counter, and I'm assuming you're Farrah Irvine." His lips quirked up in a quick smile Farrah supposed most females appreciated. He possessed a quiet handsomeness and a gentle spirit, both things that had drawn her to Darren too.

"I am," she said, opening the rear door. "I brought groceries to make dinner. He's supposed to be here for the lesson." She picked up the bags and headed up the sidewalk.

"I'm Cody." He came down the steps and took the bags of groceries from her. "And I doubt Darren will back before nightfall. He was…in a mood when he went out, and he saddled Paintbrush and took a backpack."

Nightfall. That was at least five hours from now. Could Farrah spend five hours on this farm without Darren's comforting hand in hers? Her throat closed as Cody opened the door and waited for her to enter the farmhouse first.

She steeled herself and straightened her shoulders before walking inside. Absolutely everything and nothing was the same as she remembered it. The new owner—a man named Tucker Jenkins—hadn't done any home improvements. The furniture was different, but the walls were still whitewashed, and the nail hole where a picture of her and the male junior champion had hung above the fireplace remained.

Farrah rubbed her arms as if cold, glancing around like ghosts would come swooping up the stairs and engulf her in sharp knives and spiders.

"You could get started," Cody said. "Or I could take you around the farm."

"No," Farrah said quickly. She definitely didn't want a tour of the place she knew like the back of her hand. She didn't want to see how much it had changed while also staying the same. "I'll just get started on dinner."

Maybe the scent of pork chops with onion gravy would entice Darren in from wherever he'd gone.

Please let him forgive me one more time, she prayed as she started removing ingredients from plastic bags. *Give me the strength to finally be honest with him.*

But Farrah had never felt so weak. At least she had five onions to chop to hide her tears.

CHAPTER SEVEN

Ben let Darren ride without speaking for about a half an hour. Only the sound of their horses moving through the forest grass and Rambo's panting as he darted through the trees and then came back to them met Darren's ears.

Then Ben asked, "When are you going to move past Farrah?"

Darren growled, though the question had real merit.

"Sam said you saw her at the cemetery weeks ago," Ben said, peering over at Darren in an annoying way. "You're not dating her again, are you?"

"I wish." Darren could sum up everything he felt with those two words. If they were dating, they'd at least be talking. Sharing important things. Working through problems. This constant struggle with *what to say, how to say it, should he even say it?* was exhausting.

He sighed, unsure if he really wanted to date Farrah again. He just wanted to stop this emotional cycle of turmoil. Wanted to stop dreaming about her. Wanted to find someone else to occupy his mind and time.

But that would take a very, very long time, and Darren knew it. But if the pain throbbing from his heart throughout his whole body dimmed a little bit each day, he'd take it. Eventually, it would have to stop, Darren knew that. He'd felt the same way after learning his parents had both died in the same plane crash.

And now, twelve years later, he could look at pictures of them, think of them, without the same level of heartache.

Ben whistled a tune their father used to, and Darren let his frustration and annoyance float away, up into the brilliant blue Vermont sky.

"I don't know how to move past her," he finally admitted.

"Because you don't *want* to move past her."

Darren nodded, his chest heaving with the effort it took for him to contain his emotion. No, he didn't want to move past her.

"I'm in love with her." His voice sounded like he'd gargled with nails. "I never told her, but I still love her." He scoffed at his own stupidity. "And I hate that I can't figure out how to stop, and now she's working out at the Bybees, and—"

He sucked in a breath to get himself to stop babbling. He wasn't prepared to tell Ben about his time out at Jim and Corey's farm, not right now. He nudged Paintbrush away from the ferns he loved and kept the horse moving through the forest away from the farm. He whistled for Rambo, who'd wandered off again, and the dog came bounding through the bushes.

Ben glanced at him and looked away, an unreadable look on his face. Darren hoped he wouldn't ask about the Bybees right now, and relief poured through him when Ben didn't.

"So I guess it's probably not a good time to tell you our news," Ben said.

Darren had noticed how Ben had started talking in the plural "we" and "our" since getting married. It was as annoying as it was cute, and Darren longed for the day when he was part of a "we" and an "our."

"Sure it is," Darren said. Then they wouldn't have to talk about him. He wouldn't have to take advice from his younger brother. He wouldn't have to try to figure out a way to live his life without Farrah in it.

"Rae's pregnant," he said, joy bubbling through his throat. "She's due in January."

An explosion ripped through Darren, mostly made of happiness for Ben and Rae. Some jealousy coated his insides, but thankfully, none of that bled into his hearty, "Congratulations, Ben. That is great news."

Ben laughed, the boisterous sound pushing through the trees around them. "For a while there, she wasn't sure she could have a baby, so we're relieved. She's been pretty sick, but she's starting to feel better now, and the doctor said the baby looks healthy and is growing properly."

"That's great," Darren said, his mind catching on the

bit of information that his brother and his wife might not have been able to have a baby. Darren hadn't known that. Ben had never said anything. Darren swallowed back the thought that if he hadn't been so wrapped up in his own problems, he might have been able to be a better support for Ben.

"Well, I better get back," Ben said. "I told Rae I'd pick up dinner on the way home." He swung his horse around, and Darren hesitated. He'd brought out his overnight pack, and he was prepared to stay out in the woods with his horse and his dog.

But did he really want to?

"You stayin' out here?" Ben looked over his shoulder. "I don't think you should. Come on back to the house and come to dinner with me and Rae."

Darren didn't know how to tell his brother that eating dinner as the third wheel wasn't exactly appealing. He shook his head. "I'll come back, but I'm not going to dinner with you two."

Ben gave him a knowing smile and nodded, waiting until Darren swung his horse around too. "Let's go, Rambo."

"You and that dog." Ben chuckled.

"Hey, he's all I have." Darren managed to smile to take some of the sting out of the words. "We both miss Logan, so we've bonded. That's all."

"Or you've gone soft for a paw pal."

Darren laughed with his brother, because he didn't dare admit that he simply needed a companion, and if all he could get was a furry, four-legged friend, he'd take it.

Darren knew something was amiss as soon as he broke through the trees on the edge of the farthest field from the farmhouse. Something sweet and savory filled the air, and it only took him three deep breaths to identify it.

"Farrah," he whispered.

"What?" Ben asked.

"Farrah's here." He swung wildly toward his brother. "Why would she be here?"

Confusion furrowed Ben's brow. "How do you know it's her?"

"She has this pork chop recipe she makes for me." His voice broke on the last two words, but he'd be able to identify the salty, tangy scent of the onion gravy from the grave.

Before Ben could answer, his phone chimed several times. He bent over it, the lines between his eyebrows disappearing as he read. "You're right. Farrah's here."

"Who was that?"

"Cody. Apparently she wanted to give you a cooking lesson at four-thirty."

Darren cursed himself for leaving his phone in the kitchen, but he supposed it wouldn't have mattered. He wouldn't have gotten any calls or texts from her out in the forest, just like Ben hadn't gotten Cody's messages until they were back on the farm.

"What time is it?"

"Just after five." Ben swung down off his horse. "I'll put Paintbrush away if you want to go in."

Darren faced the farmhouse, at war with himself once again. He finally shook his head. "No, I'll take care of Willow for you. You have a pregnant wife to get home to."

Ben practically wore the pregnant glow on his face, and he handed his mare's reins to Darren. "Don't take too long," he said. "And go talk to Farrah. Tell her how you feel. You might be surprised how well that works."

Darren nodded and grunted his consent, but he would absolutely not be telling Farrah that he loved her. After all, some secrets should be taken to the grave.

He methodically worked through Willow and Paintbrush's care, taking an extra moment to run his hand down his horse's nose before facing the back of the farmhouse. Every cell in his body vibrated, and he took several deep breaths.

Be nice to her.

He appreciated that his oldest brother's words were there in his head. He'd have preferred his father, but Sam had done everything in his power to make sure the other boys hadn't wanted for anything.

Darren walked toward the house deliberately, his footsteps slow and sure. When the night ended, he wanted someone to tell about the forthcoming encounter with Farrah. All at once, Darren realized that some of the responsibility of maintaining a relationship with his brothers fell on him.

He couldn't expect them to plan everything, always call or text first, ask questions about his life. It was a two-way street—and the very reason he'd been so frustrated with Farrah these past few weeks.

He felt like he was trying. Saying all the right things, and giving her space, and letting her come to him.

And she hadn't come to him.

Until now.

He pulled open the back door and got hit square in the face with the scent of browning pork and starchy potatoes and butter. "Hello?" he called. He couldn't quite believe that Farrah had come to Steeple Ridge. She *never* had before. Insisted she wouldn't.

Scraping from the kitchen sounded and then Cody peered around the corner. "Oh, hey, Darren." He spoke too loud to be casual, and he wore a panicked look on his face. Before he could say anything else, Farrah joined him.

Hope shone in her teal eyes, sucker-punching Darren again. "You're late," she said like it was no big deal that she'd come to this farm where she'd claimed she'd never step foot again.

Darren didn't know how to respond, so he simply stepped past the pair of them and moved into the kitchen.

"I've just started peeling the potatoes." Farrah edged around him without actually touching him, but the electricity from her nearness practically shocked him. "So let me show you that." Her nervousness was a palpable being in the air, and Darren didn't know what to do with it. How to erase it.

"Is this part of the lesson?" he asked.

"Yes. You missed the onion chopping, but I showed Cody so he can teach you."

Darren exchanged a glance with Cody, who now wore a grin the size of the Mississippi River. He made a shooing motion as if Darren wasn't already standing in the kitchen with Farrah and made a show of stomping downstairs.

"Wash your hands first."

Darren followed her directions and stood beside her as she peeled a potato. "You try it." She handed the peeler to him, and he picked up a potato with the skin still on. It felt small in his large hand, but he managed to get the blades of the peeler across it.

"I have water here." She indicated the steaming pot already on the stove. "It has quite a bit of salt in it, because potatoes taste like nothing, so you have to flavor them."

He nodded, not quite trusting his voice to work properly.

"We caramelized the onions and married them with beef stock. Then I browned the chops and stuck them in the oven while the gravy reduces. Four hundred degrees."

Darren went along with her though words like *caramelized* and *browned* and *reduces* were quite advanced culinary vocabulary for him.

He did manage to pick up a knife and get the potatoes in similar-sized cubes. Farrah put them all into the now-boiling water at the same time and stepped back. "Now we usually do a vegetable, but you rarely eat anything green, so I didn't bring anything tonight."

"I think we have frozen peas." They were probably left from when Sam used to make dinner a year ago, and Darren had no idea how to take them from rock hard to edible, but he stepped toward the refrigerator anyway.

"It's fine," Farrah said.

"Oh, I forgot." Darren froze, now only a foot from her. "You don't like peas." He gazed down on her, her peachy-pink skin a bit sun-kissed from her work on the farm these past few weeks. His natural instinct to take her in his arms, lean down, and kiss her reared so high he flinched toward her.

Instead of touching her, he whispered, "I miss you."

He expected her to jump back, grab her keys, and disappear out the front door.

She closed her eyes and nodded slightly. "I miss you too."

He took both of her hands in his, a rush of adrenaline shooting through him at the skin-to-skin contact. "Why'd you come to the farm tonight?"

She lifted her chin. "To apologize. Something I should've done a long time ago."

"For what?"

"I haven't been exactly forthcoming with things," she said, her voice low and barely audible.

Darren held very still, as he'd known she hadn't told him everything about her past, her life, herself. He'd been fine with the pieces she had given him, because he believed that was why they'd been dating—they'd been getting to know each other one little bit at a time.

A tremor of fear shook his voice when he said, "Like what?"

She pressed her lips together, and they burst with a dark shade of pink when she stopped. "Let's eat first, and then I'll tell you."

He wasn't sure he'd be able to swallow a single bite with her right there in the farmhouse. Right there in the farmhouse, holding his hand. Talking to him. Gazing up at him like she wanted him to kiss her the way he used to.

He fell back a step, then two, and dropped her hands. "All right. How long until dinner's ready?"

CHAPTER EIGHT

Farrah choked down half a pork chop and a few mouthfuls of mashed potato before she leaned away from her plate. Darren didn't seem to be in his usual eat-anything mode, because he finished only moments after her.

Without speaking, she stood and collected both of their plates. The sink was the same as it had been when she used to stand next to Jamie and get lessons on how to bake chocolate chip cookies.

She turned away from the memory and said, "I used to sleep in the bedroom at the top of the stairs sometimes."

Darren jolted like she'd connected him to a live wire and sent a hundred volts through him. "You did?"

"I participated in horse shows out here all the time. I had lessons every day after school. I was the female junior champion for four straight years. Sometimes, on the weekends or in the summer, I'd just stay here instead of going back into town." The words spilled from her like water over a dam, flooding out and staining the lowlands surrounding it.

"I sleep in the bedroom at the top of the stairs," he said, his voice strangled and hoarse.

Farrah's blood turned to ice for two heartbeats, and then raced like hot lava through her veins. "Are the walls still purple?"

He shook his head. "Pale blue."

"Ah. Someone painted then." She swallowed, everything in her urging her to flee this place, but the man in front of her was begging her to stay, to tell him everything. Reaching for his hand, she said, "Let's go for a walk, and I'll tell you everything."

Her hand fit in his like they were nesting dolls. His large and all-encompassing, hers just small enough to fit inside comfortably. The warmth from his skin sent chills along her shoulders and down her arms. She'd spoken true when she'd said she missed him, and she could feel his emotions for her in the personal bubble that surrounded him.

A dog waited by the back door, perking up when Darren exited the house. "C'mon, boy," he said, holding out his hand for the Australian shepherd to sniff. He ambled to his feet and trotted along beside them.

Farrah faced the fields, the barn, the show arena. She drew a deep breath of the country evening air that had so often soothed her. "I loved this place." She noticed the past tense use of love, and she was sure Darren did too, but he said nothing.

"How many horses do you have right now?"

"We're slow in the summer," he said.

"Jamie used to be about half-full in the summer."

"That's about where we are."

So twenty horses or so. Their feet crunched on the gravel as they left the backyard and walked parallel to the back barn. "Personal horses still kept in the back here?"

"Yep."

"Want to show me yours?"

Darren stilled and studied her, and Farrah hated that she'd never let him introduce her to his horse. That was a big deal for a cowboy, and she'd flat-out refused to do it. "I'm sorry," she whispered. "I want to meet him, Darren."

He reached up and touched her lips with his forefinger, sending her emotions reeling and her hopes toward the heavens.

"You never say my name," he said, closing his eyes. "Say it again." He cocked his head as if listening for a great secret or a hidden sound.

"I'd like to meet your horse, Darren."

A smile tugged at the corners of his mouth, drawing her attention there. The gravitational pull between them intensified until Farrah thought sure she'd snap in half. He opened his eyes and said, "Let's go meet him then."

He led her into the back barn, which had seen a remodel since the last time she'd been here. The stall walls were all new, with chalkboards hanging beside each one to hold the horse's name.

"Paintbrush," she read aloud as he opened the stall door. A beautiful horse greeted him with a snuffle and a huff. He was tall and the color of cream, except for a few markings in red along his hooves and tail, as if he'd stepped in paint.

Darren explained that he'd earned the horse on a ranch in Nevada and hauled him all the way here in a rented trailer and truck. He obviously loved the horse, and the horse loved him.

Farrah stoked his neck. "He's beautiful."

"Thanks."

"I used to have a horse named Evita," she said, her mind flowing back to the black mare easily. "She was the best jumper. She could go over anything, into anything. She was fearless."

Like Farrah was trying to be.

She sighed and turned her back to the stalls, leaning into the wood. "I sold her to a girl just younger than me when I quit."

Darren tucked a strand of her hair behind her ear, a loving, gentle gesture that nearly undid Farrah's composure. "Why did you quit?"

Fear kept Farrah's vocal chords silent. She didn't want to tell him, while at the same time she hoped telling someone would free her from the chains she'd been wearing for so long.

"Come on." She took his hand again and led him out of the barn and toward the show arena. "My parents never missed an event," she said. "My dad drove me everywhere and anywhere I needed to go." Her tongue only tripped slightly on the words *my dad*. She didn't think Darren noticed. "We used to live in Island Park, so we had our own pastures and barns and stables."

They passed the storage shed which used to hold equipment and winter feed. She reached the fence that separated the hay fields from the show stadium and put one foot on the bottom rung.

"I rode and showed and won for a couple of years after high school. I thought I was going to be a champion rider and then a breeder. I thought I'd work at Steeple Ridge, and live in Island Park, forever." She released his hand and leaned her elbows on the top of the fence.

Darren smartly gave her a few inches of space as he gazed out into the show arena too.

"Then one day, after I'd won an event that put me in the top qualifiers for a national championship, my father and I were the last ones here. He brought me right here." Her throat narrowed, and Farrah closed her eyes to relive the short conversation they'd had.

She turned to break the memory threatening to crush the life out of her. "He told me that he wasn't my real father. That my mother wasn't my biological mother. That they hadn't been able to have children, and that I was adopted."

Farrah drew in a deep breath, her eyes never leaving Darren's. To his credit, he didn't gasp or sigh or react other than to breathe with her.

"I had no idea. I looked like my father. I acted like my

mother. Everyone commented on it all the time. But I suddenly felt…lost. Alone. Abandoned." Her chest shuddered. "Completely unwanted and unloved, though it makes no sense. My parents had showered me with love, given me anything I wanted."

She absently rubbed her hands up and down her arms, and Darren took her into a warm embrace. "I started questioning everything. Who I was. What I really liked. Where I'd come from. I *needed* to know." She sighed into his chest, the solid security of it like a balm to her weary soul. "So I quit riding. It was something I thought me and my dad shared because of genetics, but it wasn't. I went to college for a couple of years, and then I decided to try acting."

"Across the country," he murmured.

"My real father was a producer," she said. "I'd tracked him down enough to know that."

"Did you find him?"

She nodded, the tears gathering in her eyes now. She was proud she'd held them back for so long. "And he didn't want me." Her emotion spilled over and tears splashed down her cheeks. She shrugged, though nothing about what she was saying was inconsequential.

Farrah pulled in a ragged breath and clung to Darren. "I felt abandoned when I learned I was adopted. Like my own parents didn't love me enough to keep me. And the parents who *had* adopted me didn't trust me enough to tell me I wasn't theirs. And when I met my biological father, and he…." She shook her head and pulled away from him. Pulled out of his comforting embrace. Pulled back all the emotion she'd allowed to leak out.

"I am unlovable," she said. "Unwanted. And I don't believe anyone will ever love me or want me." Her breath shuddered as he started to shake his head, his dark eyes ablaze with something she couldn't quite name. "I'm broken, Darren. My dad broke me, right here by this fence." She gestured to the whole of Steeple Ridge Farm behind Darren. "This place broke me, and that's why I don't ride horses anymore, and why I can't come here and be with you."

"Farrah," he started, but she shook her head.

"So I'm sorry," she continued. "I'm sorry for ever letting you think we could be together. I shouldn't have gone out with you at all, and for that, I'm so, so sorry." She hoped the depth of her apology could be heard in her tone so he would know she had never meant to hurt him.

"I have to go."

"Don't go." His voice was made of air and agony.

"I'm sorry," she said again before giving in to the insatiable urge to leave this farm and never come back.

FARRAH SPENT THE FOLLOWING DAY IN THE COMPANY OF strawberry plants and mushrooms. Meagan had called in sick, and Audra had gone up to Montpelier to browse through the biggest nursery in Vermont, leaving Farrah alone in the botanical boutique.

She started her day by checking on the fish. She felt a connection to them, and the Bybees had two groups of tilapia right now. Some that were in the main tank—the one shaded by the vertically grown strawberries—and a batch that was six weeks old and had to be fed by hand.

Farrah weighed out the food and put it in the blue barrels, watching the clock and the food consumption. These younger fish were fed as much as they would eat in thirty minutes, and Meagan expected impeccable records of how much and when the fish were fed.

Farrah thrived on procedures, and she went through the daily water checks for pH, and today she needed to do the weekly tests for ammonia levels, nitrates, and dissolved oxygen. The boutique brought in the most money for the tilapia, and Farrah had grown a soft spot in her heart for the fish.

With the aqua part of her aquaponics job done, Farrah left the shed and wandered to the tree line beyond the greenhouse. She pulled out her sandwich and ate lunch in the quiet stillness of Vermont's countryside.

She'd never felt so at peace, despite her confessions to Darren the previous day. He hadn't tried to call her last night or come over to convince her that she was lovable. This morning, though, he'd texted her a link she hadn't opened yet.

That was all. A single link. No explanation. No argument about what she'd told him. She wasn't sure what she'd been expecting his reaction to be, but a quiet acceptance of who she was and what she'd done had unsettled her.

She finished her peanut butter and peach jam sandwich and tapped on the link he'd sent. A music video popped up, and the song that started playing was one of her favorite hymns. She closed her eyes and let the music wash over her, through her, the power of the lyrics enough to move her to tears.

They were all about the Lord's love and acceptance of his children. For a long time after she'd discovered she was adopted, she'd wondered why God would allow her to feel so forgotten. To be so lost. To be abandoned by her own flesh and blood.

After a while, and after she'd stopped going to church, she realized that God didn't do things to her. He did them *for* her.

She'd slowly come back from a disastrous marriage, the wrong career choice, and the agonizing rejection of her birth father. And coming back from all of that had left her without anywhere else to go.

So she'd come home.

And coming home to Island Park had been harder than she'd expected. But going out to Steeple Ridge? That hadn't been nearly as hard as she'd expected. The same level of peace existed there. The same comfort. The sameness of the place, more than anything, reminded her of how unchangeable God was.

Am I lovable? she thought to herself. *Am I, Lord?* She sent the thoughts skyward now, hoping for an affirmation from Him.

Nothing happened, besides the playful breeze that was already blowing and the rustling of grasses somewhere beyond her sight. She tapped out a quick *Thanks* to Darren, sent the text, and went back inside the aquaponics shed to harvest butter lettuce and romaine lettuce.

She prepped the harvesting stations first, following the procedures in the binder Meagan had drilled into her. Tables got disinfected. Bags for product were labeled with stickers proclaiming their pesticide and herbicide-free contents. All the lettuces were sustainable and locally grown.

Meagan had procured contracts with grocery stores right here in Island Park, as well as Burlington, Bolton, and Middlebury. Farrah would harvest the lettuces today and spend tomorrow morning delivering them to the stores in the nearby vicinity. Because the plants were harvested with full roots intact, they were considered living and would last for up to two weeks outside of the rafts where they'd been growing for the past several weeks.

Farrah lifted the first raft of bright green butter lettuce to the cart and wheeled it into the prepared harvesting room. She carefully pulled the plants from the holes in the rafts—a long, white tray with holes in it—and placed them on a length of cheesecloth. She repeated this process until she'd emptied five rafts, which produced one hundred heads of lettuce.

She cut and carefully wrapped the roots, taking care to keep them intact and moist. She worked with sure strokes, the silence of the greenhouse soothing. Her mind wandered as she placed each head of lettuce in a labeled bag and put the finished product in a bin.

The hours passed quickly, the work exhilarating and fulfilling. With all the romaine and butter lettuce ready,

Farrah headed out for the day. Tomorrow, she'd take care of the fish again, deliver the lettuce, and transfer seedlings into the newly vacated rafts. If she had time, she'd seed more plants and put them on the vertical shelves to sprout.

She loved that there was always something to be done. Loved the vibrancy of the basil, the chives, the mint, the cilantro. The scent of the herbs buoyed her spirits, and she thanked the Lord for the opportunity to be doing this instead of fixing the pin setter for the tenth time or handing out used shoes.

Now if she could just fix things with Darren, maybe she'd be able to find a way to live free from the guilt that had been crushing her since she'd broken up with him three months ago.

She went to leave, turning back to the boutique as the light of the day started to wane. "See you tomorrow," she said to all the plants, all the fish, her voice carrying easily through the massive greenhouse.

Outside, the sky threatened to swallow her whole, but she gazed up into the vastness of it and felt the measure of her own creation. A smile spread across her face, and she took a moment to enjoy it. Enjoy the sunshine on her face and the crispness of the air. Enjoy her life.

She took a deep breath and dug through her bag for her keys before she realized Darren was sitting on the trunk of her car. He slid down, his boots thunking against the packed dirt where she'd parked.

"Dinner?" he asked, tucking his hands in his pockets and watching her with an even gaze.

"I don't know, Darren."

He took a slow step toward her, then another. Soon enough, he pierced her personal space and gazed down at her with an intensity she'd only seen a couple of other times. "You are lovable, Farrah," he said fiercely and fondly at the same time. "And I would know, because I fell in love with you."

CHAPTER
NINE

Darren couldn't believe what he'd just said. *I fell in love with you.*

"Once," he added onto the end of his statement, a little too late. He shoved his hands back in his pockets so he wouldn't sweep her into his arms and kiss her. Then she'd know he still loved her. "Let's go to dinner."

"All right."

"You want to drive?"

"No."

So Darren helped her into his truck, glad when she slid over and sat right next to him the way she used to do when she was his girlfriend. He wasn't sure what else to say to her, so he asked her about what she'd done in the boutique today.

She talked, filling the cab of his truck with the sound of her pretty voice. As the outskirts of town came into view,

Darren reached over and threaded his fingers through hers, bringing her wrist to his lips for a kiss.

Her tension wasn't hard to detect, but she didn't withdraw her hand or say anything. "I started going out to the Bybees about a year ago," he said. "Right after Sam left. It was…difficult with him gone, and Logan was dating Layla, and…." He sighed, trying to put into words what Jim and Corey had become to him.

"They accepted me, just how I was. They didn't care that I didn't talk much, and Jim taught me to whittle, and Corey kept tryin' to set me up with everyone she knew—at least until I met you." He drove slowly past the sports complex and the elementary school, both of which were vacant, at least for a few more weeks. Then school would start, and fall sports, and the heat of the day would yield to winter temperatures.

"We went out a lot," she said. "When did you go see them?"

"Whenever," he said. "I don't really remember. They, well, they're almost like my parents now." He swallowed as they arrived on Main Street. "What do you want to eat?"

"I don't care."

She never had. Farrah had always been easy-going about what they did when they were together—except for going out to Steeple Ridge. She'd made that proclamation on their first date, and though Darren had tried to change her mind several times, he'd never pressed her on it.

"Waffle house?" he asked, wishing he could cook so he had an excuse to go back to the farm and feed her there.

"Sure."

He turned on Center and went down several blocks to the waffle house. He parked but didn't get out. "I was afraid you were there to take them from me," he said, real soft like he wasn't sure he should give voice to the words.

Darren reached over and brushed an errant piece of her hair from her face. "You are so beautiful."

Farrah turned and looked at him—right at him, without any of her usual walls in place. A smile started in the corners of her mouth and pulled until she was smiling a true smile. Darren ached from the beauty of it, from the sparkle in her aqua eyes to the straight, white teeth she possessed.

"I want to know everything about you." He trailed his fingers across her bare shoulder, cataloguing the shiver that shook her back. "Not today. But whenever you feel like sharing."

"Like what?" she asked, her voice full of air.

"Like why your last name is Irvine and your father's name on the boarding paperwork is Paul Fletcher."

He wanted to know that, wanted to know who was buried in the cemetery, wanted to know where she'd gone to college, wanted to know where she'd lived in California and if she'd made it onto any movies or TV shows.

He'd realized after she'd left last night that she'd told him a lot about her childhood, but almost nothing about the last twelve years of her life. And he wanted it all.

"You're a really impatient man, you know that?" She glared at him, but the gaze didn't hold much more than aggravation.

"I am?"

"Yes." She folded her arms.

"Because I want to know who you are?" He opened his door and turned back to help her out of the truck.

"I just need more...time than most women."

"All right." They'd dated for eight months previously, and it seemed like all of his brothers had managed to fall in love and get engaged in that amount of time. But if Farrah needed to go slower, Darren could do that.

At least he thought he could. He held open the door for her, and as she slipped past, a dark look crossed her face. Darren regretted this whole conversation. He cleared his throat. "So Rambo learned a new trick this week."

Confusion raced through her eyes, and then she softened. "Oh yeah? What was it?"

Darren detailed how he'd been teaching the dog to crawl, and how he'd finally gotten it. "Bacon," Darren said. "Apparently that dog will do anything for bacon."

"Smart dog," Farrah said.

They got their waffles and the silence between them was as easy now as it had been back before their break up. Darren was grateful for that, grateful that Farrah let him hold her hand as they went back to his truck.

Thoughts of kissing her danced through his head, but he made a vow that he wouldn't do it. Not yet. She still had things to tell him, and he didn't want to be too impatient. Well, he did, but he didn't want Farrah to *think* he was being too impatient.

Things were new between them too, as he'd learned

more about her in the past few weeks than he'd known in the eight months they'd dated.

He pulled in beside her car and twisted to look at her. "Thanks for coming to dinner. I had a great time."

She reached up and cradled his face in her palm. "Me too, Darren."

"You are…wonderful," he said, not wanting to venture into four-letter-L-word territory again.

That soft smile he loved touched her lips only moments before she skated them across his cheek. He closed his eyes in pure bliss and took in a deep drag of her scent. Woodsy and earthy, with a hint of maple from the waffles.

"Maybe we can do another cooking lesson tomorrow," she said.

His eyes flew open. "You want to come out to the farm again?"

She shook her head. "Maybe you can come to my place." Hope shone in her eyes, and Darren seized onto it.

"Yeah, sure." The first time he'd kissed her had been at her house, and long after she got out and drove away, long after he'd returned to Steeple Ridge, long after he should've been asleep, all he could think about was kissing Farrah for the first time again.

FARRAH TEXTED DARREN SEVERAL TIMES THE NEXT DAY, AND it reminded him so strongly of when they were together, he wondered if they were.

"I need her to come out to the farm again," he muttered

after she'd told him what he'd be cooking that night. Her first couple of texts had detailed that she'd pick up the groceries and what time to be at her house.

He thought briefly about going out to the Bybee's farm and meeting her again, but since he'd taken off early last night, he couldn't leave his chores for the other boys today too. So he kept his head down and his hands busy.

His mind was just as occupied, circulating around ideas to get Farrah back out to Steeple Ridge, back into a saddle. Maybe she really did just need more time. Darren's impatience reared, and he tamped it down as he went down the row of horses to feed them.

Cody entered the barn with the horse Missy had been using for a group riding lesson. "Is she done with Diamond already?"

"He's hurt."

It was then that Darren noticed the horse limping, and the way Missy's golden retriever, Fritz, hovered near the horse's back right leg. Darren abandoned the feeding and went to assist with Diamond King, the tall, taupe-colored quarter horse that Missy had raised from a colt.

"I'll grab the blood stop powder," Darren said as he hurried down the aisle and into the tack room. Tucker had a vet out to the boarding stables every month, but Darren knew where the emergency supplies were. He threw open the cabinet doors and searched, finding the powder quickly and heading back to Cody.

He had the horse lashed to the rail above his stall door, and he stood next to him, muttering softly. Cody was a great cowboy that had worked on just about as many ranches and farms as Darren and his brothers had. Their father had died without a will, and the ranch they'd grown up on in Nevada had been bankrupt anyway.

They'd sold as much as they could, bought their mother a nice condo in Las Vegas, and had been bumping around the country for a few years before landing at Steeple Ridge. They reminded Darren a lot of himself, of his brothers, and he'd been glad for their company once Logan had left.

"I'm gonna put it on," Darren said, crouching behind and to the side of the horse, well out of kicking range.

Cody nodded once, kept his grip on Diamond's reins, and kept up the low talk. The horse flinched at the application of the powder, and Darren slicked away the excess along with the now-congealed blood.

"It doesn't look bad at all," he said.

Missy burst into the barn and beelined toward them.

"It's just a scratch," Darren said straightening. Relief flashed across her face, but she bent to see for herself.

"Might need a stitch," she said.

"Doc won't stitch that," Darren said. "It's right on the distal ligament." He stepped back again. "You should let me bandage it, and we'll check it every morning and evening."

"And he can't be ridden."

"He can graze," Darren said. "There's still plenty of summer left for grazing."

Missy nodded, her eyes tight. "Thank you, Darren."

Cody glanced over his shoulder. "I'll help 'im, boss. Then I'm fixin' to get into town. Is that okay?"

Missy nodded again, her attention and focus still on her beloved horse. Darren understood how she felt. He didn't know what he'd do if something happened to Paintbrush. "Did you get the lesson done?" he asked.

"Oh." She startled. "Cody, I need a replacement horse. Can you saddle Strawberry or Licorice for me and bring them out?" She tucked her hair, gave Diamond King one last pat, and headed back out of the barn in favor of the pastures beyond the barn, where the riding lessons took place.

"I've got Diamond," Darren said when Cody looked at him. His gaze moved to the door once more as someone else entered. Darren expected it to be Missy again, still fretting about her horse, but it was a different woman.

Cody's face turned the color of a boiled lobster, and he ducked his chin to his chest and practically sprinted away from Shiloh Davenport, the newest addition to the Steeple Ridge Farm family.

Darren watched him go, watched Shiloh stare at his retreating back, and then he met Shiloh's eye too. The leggy brunette had only been at Steeple Ridge for four days, and already there was some drama going on. He'd been so wrapped up in Farrah that he'd barely noticed the new cowgirl moving in, but Cody obviously had.

"Missy sent me to help," Shiloh said as she approached.

"Can you stay with Diamond?" Darren asked. "I need to go grab some supplies."

"Sure thing." Shiloh came to them from the largest working boarding stable in Tennessee—her father's farm—and she could ride, rope, and do any horse husbandry as well as anyone Darren knew. He gave her a friendly nod before moving back toward the tack room.

He returned a few minutes later and together, he and Shiloh got Diamond's leg wrapped. She led him into his stall and Darren fed him fresh hay and a bag of oats, just to spoil him a little. Shiloh tracked every move Cody made, only relaxing when he finally left the barn with Strawberry in tow.

"Did you see what happened?" Darren asked.

"Snakes," Shiloh said, turning away from the now-closed door. "Diamond got startled and backed into the troughs."

"Barbed wire there," Darren said.

"Yeah." She ran her hands up her arms as if she were cold.

"You okay?" Darren asked as he gathered the medical supplies he hadn't used.

"Yeah, fine. Why?" She peered up at him with hazel eyes that held more brown than green.

"Somethin' goin' on with you and Cody?" He tucked the excess bandages back into their box and waited.

Those eyes narrowed. "Did he say something to you?"

"Not at all."

"Then there's about as much goin' on with us as there is with you and Farrah Irvine." She cocked her left eyebrow as if to say, *Stay out of my business, Darren*, turned, and left the barn.

Darren couldn't help the chuckle that came out of his mouth. Shiloh was definitely a firecracker, and Cody was definitely going to get burned. Maybe he already had.

His phone buzzed, and he pulled it out of his pocket as he went to put away the supplies he'd used. *You like mint chocolate chip ice cream, right?*

Farrah. His smile widened, and Darren thought for the first time in a long time that he could actually smile and be happy doing it. *Right.*

An hour later, he pulled into her driveway. The scent of coffee met him on the porch, and when she pulled open the front door, he whistled appreciatively. "Don't you look nice?" He wanted to sweep her into his arms, but he rocked back on his heels instead.

Farrah wore a pair of cutoff shorts that showed so much leg Darren started to fantasize about kissing her again. She'd paired that with an off-the-shoulder blouse the same color as the sky, with white flowers stitched into the collar. He wanted to taste her skin right there, right above that neckline, and everything inside him turned to lava.

"The yard looks fantastic too," he said, hooking his thumb over his shoulder. "I don't know how you have time to do all that."

She kept an immaculate yard, and he'd been to her house on the weekend where she spent hours among the flowers while he did his best to keep up with her. He felt like that was all he'd ever be able to do: Try to keep up with Farrah Irvine.

"Thanks for coming," she said, stepping back to allow him into her house. "I hope you're ready to make a meatloaf."

He groaned and turned back to her. "Maybe we could just order in."

She shoved him in the chest, a playful, flirtatious gesture he hadn't had from her in far too long. He latched onto her wrist; their gazes locked; something heated and charged passed between them. Darren knew what it was. That spark, that chemistry, that had always existed between them. At least it hadn't died over the last few months apart.

He slowly lifted her wrist to his lips, pressing a kiss right against her pulse. "Are you making the mashed potatoes?" His voice sounded too low, too throaty, to pass off as casual.

"No, sir. I was just fixin' to sit down and relax while you made me dinner."

He groaned again, but got his feet moving toward her kitchen.

"Come on, now," she said. "I don't want to hear any complaining. A man who cooks dinner for his girlfriend is sexy. A whining man never is."

Darren froze, all his muscles seizing with one simple word. "Girlfriend?"

She came around him, faced him head-on. Farrah had never been afraid of a challenge, and Darren had always loved that about her.

"I want to try again, Darren," she said. "I messed up last time, and well, I'm hoping you'll let me try again."

Darren would give Farrah Irvine a dozen chances if she needed them. He couldn't get his voice to work, so he simply nodded. Her blue-green eyes filled with hope and turned glassy with unshed tears.

She cleared her throat and turned away from him. "All right, then. I want meatloaf and mashed potatoes in one hour. We'll go from there."

CHAPTER TEN

Farrah couldn't believe Darren hadn't kissed her after she'd told him she wanted a second chance with him. If Jim and Corey were to be believed, he'd been nothing but grumpy and moody since their break-up. Heck, she'd seen evidence of that herself.

But he'd only nodded, and she'd put the recipe on the kitchen counter. She'd then retreated to the safety of the living room. Too much heat stood in the kitchen, and none of it came from the boiling pot of water on the stove or the four-hundred-degree oven.

Darren worked methodically, which was a nice way for Farrah to say *slow*. But he got a meatloaf put together and in the oven before turning his attention to the potatoes. He'd just made those a couple of nights ago, but she still heard him muttering as he peeled.

She hated peeling potatoes with the fire of a thousand suns, so she couldn't blame him. Most of the blame she had to give always came back to herself. She had a lot more to tell him, and from what he'd said yesterday at dinner, he wasn't going anywhere until she started talking. That more than anything had shown her that he genuinely cared about her.

So go on, she told herself. *Get in there and tell him something he doesn't know.*

She leaned against the counter as he put the lid on the potatoes. "You're doing awesome, Darren."

"Thanks." He glanced around the kitchen he'd cleaned as he'd cooked. "What do I do now?"

"Nothing. Everything cooks." She glanced into her microscopic living room. "You come sit by me and talk until the timer goes off." She extended her hand toward him, and he hesitated for a moment before taking it.

She waited for him to sit, and then she curled into him the way she'd done many times before. Usually she kissed him first. No, usually they ate first. Then he kissed her until she couldn't breathe, then he fell asleep on her couch while they watched a movie.

Tonight, there was no food yet, no kissing, and no movie.

Farrah drew in a deep breath. "I haven't talked to my parents in a while," she admitted.

Darren drew lazy patterns along her bare arms, eliciting a shiver from her. "Why not?"

"I'm...I'm not their daughter."

His fingers stilled. "Farrah," he said in a warning tone. "Yes, you are. They raised you. You're their daughter."

"You don't understand." She shook her head, not quite sure what response she'd expected from him.

"Help me understand."

Farrah didn't say anything. She couldn't articulate the way she felt well enough for him to understand. She wasn't sure she understood it.

"I felt betrayed," she said. "They lied to me for almost two decades."

Darren resumed the upward slide of his fingers. He left fire everywhere he touched, and Farrah settled deeper into his side. "Did they say why?"

"My dad said they were trying to protect me."

"From what?"

"From the truth: That I was unwanted."

Darren sucked in a breath. "Farrah, they wanted you. They still do."

She wanted him to say he wanted her. She waited, but he didn't say it.

"You should call them," he said instead. "Have you been up to see them? Do they even know you're back?"

"Of course," she said. "I've been to see them once."

"In a year."

"And they came here for lunch once."

"Two visits in twelve months." He shifted, twisting to look at her. She could only meet his intense gaze for three seconds before looking away. "Do you call your mom?" he asked, his voice gentle and rough at the same time.

Farrah shook her head as shame filled her.

"Farrah," he said. "Maybe you need…help."

"Like a therapist?"

"Yeah." He tucked her into his side again. "It's not normal to feel this way, sweetheart. Your father told you about your adoption twelve years ago. You should be able to go see your parents, call your mom on the phone all the time. It's not normal not to."

What did he know about being normal? He didn't have parents. "You don't understand, because your mom and dad aren't here."

He stiffened, his grip on her bicep no longer loving and sincere but a vice. "That's exactly why I understand, Farrah. Don't you know how lucky you are to have them here with you? How can you waste a single day by not talking to them?"

The timer on the meatloaf went off, and Darren stood. "I can't believe you have two people who love you so much that they adopted you when you didn't even come from them, and you won't even talk to them. It's—it's—" He opened the oven and pulled out the meatloaf, practically dropping it on the stovetop. "It's selfish, Farrah."

She stood too, his reaction so not what she'd needed or expected. "Don't tell me I'm selfish."

"What would you call it?" He cocked one hip while still wearing the oven mitt, and dang, if Farrah didn't find him amusing and charming and downright attractive all at the same time.

"I don't know," she said. Maybe she did need professional help.

"All I know is that if my parents were still here, I'd call them all the time," he said. "I'd probably still be living in Wyoming on our farm, and I wouldn't have had to traipse all over this country trying to find a job that would support me. My brothers and I—" His voice cut off as if someone had pressed mute on his vocal chords.

He shook his head, his eyes bright and dark simultaneously. "I miss my mom and dad terribly," he said, all the words sticking in his throat. "They're not here to do anything about it. But yours are. Don't you miss your mom and dad?"

She did. Oh, she did. She finally nodded, the lump in her throat at his raw emotion too big to swallow past.

"You're pushy," she said.

"And impatient, I've been told." He gazed evenly at her. "What are you going to do about it?"

"I don't know what to say to them."

"You're a smart woman, Farrah. You'll figure it out." Darren turned to drain the potatoes while every emotion Farrah had ever experienced streamed through her. He *was* pushy and impatient, but maybe he was also right. At least about this.

Why did you tell him if you didn't want him to lecture you? Because Farrah had known he would. Darren was kind, and caring, and gentle, but he was also loyal, and honest, and true. He said what needed to be said. He forgave easily.

Steam lifted above his head, and Farrah rushed up behind him and embraced him. "I'm sorry," she whispered against his back.

He turned carefully in her arms. "Don't be sorry to me." He wiped her tears and cradled her face. "Want me to stay with you while you call your parents?"

She thought about the meatloaf, getting cold on the stove. She thought about the potatoes, which wouldn't steam forever.

She nodded. "Would you?"

"Of course." He lowered his head, and she thought sure he'd kiss her. He did, but not on the mouth where she wanted him to, where she could connect with him too. Instead, his lips brushed along her cheek, pressed against her temple, and lifted lightly away from her.

She held very still in his arms, the scent of his cologne, and horses, and the starch from the potatoes mingling in her nose.

"Do you want to eat first?" he asked. "Or after you call them?"

Farrah wasn't sure she could stomach a single bite of food. "After," she said, trying to absorb the strength and solidity from Darren before he released her.

She retreated into the living room to collect her phone, and when she turned to face him, she changed her mind. "I want to call them by myself."

"That's fine." He advanced toward her, a look of acceptance and love on his face. "I'll take Bolt into the backyard."

"You hate Bolt." Her smile shook, but she didn't care. Darren was here, and he wasn't running away from her. He hadn't liked how she'd acted, but he hadn't condemned her for it either. She could only hope and pray her parents would be as forgiving.

"We get along fine." He scooped the gray tabby cat into his huge arms to the symphony of a hiss and left Farrah to herself. She watched him set the cat in the grass and settle into the hammock he'd installed last spring. They'd spent many evenings in that hammock, their legs tangled as they talked and kissed and made plans for the future.

Plans she wanted to resume. A future she wanted to have with him.

She squared her shoulders and dialed her mother's number. After all, Darren wouldn't want to be with her if she didn't clear the air with her family.

"Farrah?" her mom asked. "Is that you, honey?"

Farrah's emotions cracked, and tears rushed from her eyes. "Hey, Mom," she said. "Can you get Dad on the phone too? I want to talk to both of you."

Shuffles and scuffs came through the line, and then her dad said, "Farrah, is that you?"

The fact that they'd both asked if it was truly her, like they couldn't believe she'd called, made her heart twist in her chest.

"It's me," she said, her mind still blank. But maybe she didn't need to speak with her mind. Maybe she should let her heart take over. "I love you guys," she said, her voice barely more than a whisper. "I'm so sorry I've treated you badly all these years. Can you ever forgive me?"

A sob came through the line, and then her mom said, "Of course, honey. We love you too."

"We love you, Farrah," her dad said, and Farrah nodded though they couldn't see her, tears streaming down her face.

CHAPTER
ELEVEN

August melted into September, which promised cooler temperatures and less horses to take care of now that the summer riding lessons had ended. But there was still plenty to do around the farm as they prepared for winter. Outbuildings to repair. Fields to harvest. Stalls to clean and prep for the clients who would bring their horses by Halloween. Sometimes earlier, if Mother Nature decided to snow in early fall.

Darren loved his work on the farm. Tucker paid well, because he knew his men needed a way to support themselves and possibly a family.

Darren had started thinking a lot about a family again now that he and Farrah were dating again. He still hadn't kissed her, but he'd been watching her for the go-ahead signal. He didn't want to be pushy and impatient with her, so they spent time in restaurants, in the botanical boutique, at her place.

One day in mid-September, he asked Cody and Shiloh to finish his chores for him so he could go visit Jim and Corey. He'd been out to the farm, of course, but his time had been occupied by Farrah, and he missed his conversations with Corey and his whittling with Jim.

He pulled up to the house and got out of his truck, taking in all the colored and fallen leaves Jim hadn't gotten to yet. He bypassed the front porch and went around to the shed in the backyard to get a rake.

He pulled the leaves into neat piles and had the front yard finished before Jim made an appearance. "You don't have to rake my leaves." He leaned against the porch railing, those overalls and that gray T-shirt ever-present.

"I sure don't." Darren leaned the rake against the trunk of a tree and climbed the steps. Jim looked tired, and concern spiked in Darren's chest. "You okay?"

"Had a bit of bronchitis," he said, easing into his chair. "You want to carve today?"

"Yes, sir."

Jim pointed to a basket in the corner. "Make me something nice."

Darren chose a piece of wood and collected his knife from his glove box. He stroked the blade across the bark, the silence between him and Jim comforting and calming.

"So you're seein' Farrah again."

"Yes, sir."

"You like that woman a lot." He wasn't asking, and Darren had been honest with Jim and Corey before. He didn't kiss and tell, but he'd used them as a sounding board, asked them questions about falling in love, relied on their support as if they were his parents.

"I'm in love with her." He just said it right out loud for the world to hear. He hoped she was way back in the boutique, behind the fish tanks, so she didn't hear.

"Corey was right then."

"Did she tell you that?"

"She did." Jim picked up his knife and selected a piece of wood. His shavings joined Darren's on the porch. "I'm worried about you, bud."

Darren slowed his knife and paused to look at Jim. "Why?"

"She broke your heart once before, and I can't watch you go through that again." The unadulterated love in his eyes made Darren's chest tight, tighter.

"You're like a son to me, Darren." Jim's knife went swish swish swish against the wood. "I want you to be happy."

Darren stared at the older gentleman, pure love flowing through him. "You're like a dad to me, Jim."

Jim looked up and their eyes met. Darren felt everything for Jim he'd ever felt for his own father. He nodded and focused back on his wood. "She makes me happy," he finally said, his throat quite narrow.

"You think this time she'll see it through to the end?"

"She's not a bad person," Darren said, the need to defend her strong. "She's…."

"Broken," Jim supplied. "I know. We can see it."

"She's getting help." The face he saw in his mind

started to take shape. He nicked out a piece of wood for the eye on one side, then the other. "She's fixing things with her parents, and she's seeing a therapist every week now."

She still didn't tell him much, but Darren had employed every patient bone and cell and blood vessel he owned. It had only been a few weeks since her complete break-down in her kitchen. They never did eat the meatloaf, and he never had mashed the potatoes. She'd come out to the hammock with water pouring from every hole on her face, and he'd held her tight until she'd quieted.

Then he'd stayed for another hour. He'd tucked her into bed, fed her cat, and slipped out like a thief in the night. Problem was, it was his heart that had been stolen that night. He loved her, and he'd do anything to protect her, shelter her, ease her pain.

And he liked being her protector, loved the vulnerability she allowed herself to show only to him. He thought they really could make things work between them, given enough time.

"She just needs time," Darren said aloud, as much for himself as for Jim.

"And you've got loads of that."

"Yes, sir." Darren held the face out to examine it. He added a few more lines for the hair and then he held it out for Jim to see. "This is my father."

Jim stopped his carving and took the whittled face from Darren. He looked at the chin and then sized up Darren's. "He looks a lot like you."

"Me and Logan got most of his genes," he said. "Ben and Sam looked more like my mother."

Jim extended the piece back, and then faltered. "Can I have this?"

Surprise shot through Darren. "Sure."

Jim smiled at it and then Darren. "Should we go see what Corey's made for dinner? Or are you and Farrah going out again?"

Darren stood and gazed out at the piles of leaves. "I'll bag these and be right in. Farrah's busy with her family tonight, and I'd love to stay for dinner." And not only because he wasn't cooking. Farrah had insisted he cook three times a week at her house, and Darren was becoming quite adept with chicken, potatoes, roasts, and he'd even used a pressure cooker recently.

With the leaves bagged and ready for pickup, he went inside to find Jim and Corey standing side-by-side at the island. She laughed at something he said, and his arm settled around her waist.

Darren watched the picture of love before him, a strong desire to have it in his own life roaring forward. He still hadn't even kissed Farrah since their break-up. And he knew where he wanted to do it: Steeple Ridge.

It was time she started making some new memories of that place.

"Hey." He cleared his throat as he entered the kitchen. The scent of oranges and peanut oil met his nose. "Just the three of us?"

"I thought we'd just eat at the bar." Corey indicated the

three plates she'd set on the far side of the island from where she and Jim stood. "How are you, dear?" She embraced Darren, who closed his eyes and imagined his own mother and how she would hug him every morning before sending him off to school.

"Great." His voice caught in his throat. He and Jim exchanged a glance, and Darren pulled back from Corey. "So you and Jim have been talkin' about me."

She shot a look to her husband. "Out of love, Darren. We only want you to be happy."

"I know." He glanced at the orange chicken and brown rice on the stove. "So is this ready? I'm starving."

Corey laughed, her tight black curls bouncing with the movement. "Say grace, then."

Darren did, and they loaded their plates with food and sat at the bar. "So I might have some questions for you, if you don't mind."

"About Farrah?"

"Sort of. I want…she won't come out to Steeple Ridge, and I need her out there."

Corey simply speared another piece of broccoli, and Jim's silence wasn't abnormal.

Darren sighed and gazed at his food. "She has bad memories of the place. It's where I work. I love it there, and I want her to love it there."

"She's a good rider," Jim said, like that had anything to do with what Darren had said.

"Any ideas of how I can build better memories for her at Steeple Ridge?"

Corey, for the first time in Darren's recollection of her,

was speechless. Jim just shrugged. "She likes aquaponics," he said. "Maybe you should build a small commercial operation at Steeple Ridge and ask her to help you do it."

"Don't be ridiculous," Corey said, swatting his arm. She peered around Jim to Darren. "I don't know, dear, but I'll keep thinking."

Darren nodded, Jim's idea swimming around in his head like the thousands of tilapia in the tanks down in the boutique.

Maybe building an aquaponics unit wasn't such a bad idea. Of course, he'd have to get Missy and Tucker on board, and that wouldn't be easy….

Darren shelved the idea, finished dinner with his two favorite people, and headed back to his own farm. Farrah belonged on a farm—one with horses *and* fish. Every time Darren thought about her riding a horse, his breath got stuck in his lungs.

Why do you want a dream for her she doesn't even want? he asked himself, not for the first time.

He'd just pulled up to the farmhouse at Steeple Ridge when his phone rang.

"Ben, hey," he said, his heart lighter than it had been in months. "What's up?"

Nothing came through the line, and Darren checked his phone. Call still connected. "Ben?"

"It's Rae," he said, his voice high and choked. "She's been in an accident, and she's at the hospital, and they won't let me see her."

"I'm on my way."

The hospital in Island Park sat right next to Peacock

Park. Darren only knew that, because Logan had told him all about the birds that lived there. And about how Layla had kissed him there in the rain.

Darren had only listened with one ear then, but he knew enough to know he could park at the park and get into the hospital quicker than using their underground system.

"Reagan Buttars," he asked the information desk.

"She's in emergency," the woman said, and Darren took off down the hall. He found Ben in a waiting room, his face the perfect picture of agony. "Ben, hey." The brothers embraced, and Ben's shoulders shook.

Horrible flashbacks quaked through Darren. Sam coming home to tell them their parents had died. Waking Ben last. All the brothers crying. Before, it had been Sam who was the strong one. Sam who took care of everything. Sam who kept the family together, and food on the table, and bills paid.

Darren needed to call his brother and thank him for what he'd done. But right now, he needed to be the strong one for Ben.

"What happened?" he asked. They took two seats and Darren watched his brother closely.

"Car accident," he said. "She was coming out to the farm to pick me up, and I guess she went to pass this tractor and there was another car coming." He shook his head. "Missy's family is coming from Burlington. They'll fill this place up." He cracked a smile that quickly sagged again. "I can't lose her, Darren." Tears started anew. "What if I lose her?"

Darren swallowed, his brother's agony too much for him to bear. "What have they told you?"

"That they don't know anything, and as soon as the doctor can come out to talk to me, he will."

"How long have you been here?"

"Twenty minutes."

"How did you get here?" Darren wasn't sure why all these questions mattered, but they seemed to be calming Ben.

"Cody brought me."

As if on cue, Cody came around the corner, two cups of coffee in his hand. He gave one to Ben and extended the other to Darren.

"It's yours, isn't it?" Darren asked.

"I can go get more."

Darren waved him off. "No, you drink it." He stood and moved to the other side of Ben. "Sit down."

Cody sat, and Darren cursed himself for not being at the farm that evening. He could've been there to help Ben when he needed it.

"Where's Farrah?" Ben asked. "Weren't you going to see her this afternoon?" He glanced from Cody to Darren.

"No," Darren said. "She's meeting her family tonight." They had a group therapy session Darren couldn't wait to hear all about. But he hadn't told Ben about any of that, out of respect for Farrah and her privacy.

"So where were you?"

Darren swallowed, suddenly wishing for the hot coffee so he had something to occupy his hands, give himself a few extra seconds to think.

Don't lie, he thought.

"I was out at the Bybee farm," he said, a sense of dread filling him. "I go there a lot. Jim Bybee's taught me how to whittle, and Corey feeds me whenever I come."

Ben's eyebrows shot straight up. "The Bybee farm?" He looked at Cody, clearly confused.

"Don't be mad, okay? I started going there last summer after Sam moved. I was lonely, and you guys were all dating and getting married, and Jim and Corey, they're like…the mom and dad we don't have. They've become my family." Darren silently begged him to understand.

He wasn't sure if he did or not, because a doctor came out and called, "Ben Buttars?" which caused Ben to shoot to his feet and hurry away.

Darren met Cody's eye, who simply shrugged. "Sounds nice, that Bybee farm."

"It is." Darren watched the emotion play across Cody's face. "You and Wade should come with me next time I go."

"How often do you go?"

"Whenever. There's not a schedule."

Cody started nodding. He sipped his coffee. "I'd like that. I sure do miss my mom sometimes. But she's got herself a new husband and a new life, and Wade and I just don't fit."

"I'm sure that's not—"

"So I'd like to go next time," Cody said over him, his eyes sharp.

Darren nodded, a wicked thought occurring to him. "All right. But first you have to tell me what's goin' on with you and Shiloh Davenport." He sat back in his seat as horror and then resignation flashed through Cody's eyes. "Corey's gonna get the whole story out of you anyway. Probably during the first dinner. She's gifted like that."

"Maybe I don't want to go then," Cody mumbled.

Ben called Darren's name, and he gave the other cowboy one last look before saying, "Thank you for bringing Ben into town," and going to join his brother.

"Rae's okay," Ben said. He'd wiped his face and steeled his shoulders. "The doctor said I can go back and see her now. She's asleep and probably will be for a while."

"What happened?" Darren asked as they squirted hand sanitizer into their palms and followed the doctor down a sterile hall.

"Broken leg," he said. "They took her into emergency surgery, because they thought she had some internal bleeding, but she doesn't. She's okay."

"And the baby?"

"Distressed," the doctor said over his shoulder. "But stable."

Darren put his arm around Ben and squeezed his shoulder. "That's great news, brother."

Ben nodded and stepped to the doorway the doctor indicated. He drew in a deep breath and entered the room. Darren followed, touched by the gentle and loving way Ben held Rae's hand and bent over to press a kiss to her forehead.

He'd seen so many examples of love in his life, and he tilted his chin toward the ceiling and simply thought, *Thank you.*

A commotion behind him made him turn and check out

the doorway. "Uh, Ben? I think Missy's family just arrived." And at the front of the loud, Italian-looking mob, strode Missy herself.

"I'll take care of them." Darren slipped into the hall and closed the door behind him. "Hey, Missy, she's okay." He held up both of his hands in placation, glancing at the doctor for help. But he simply looked like he'd just witnessed a terrible crime.

"Let's go out into the waiting room," Darren said.

"I want to see her."

"She's asleep. Ben's with her. She needs to rest." He shot a glance at the doctor, silently begging him to say something. "For the baby."

That got Missy moving in the opposite direction, and where she went, her family followed, so Darren led her back to the waiting room like the Pied Piper. Cody jumped to his feet and scanned the large crowd, shock covering his exhaustion.

Darren's phone went off, but he couldn't pick up Farrah's call right then. By the time he wrangled the crowd, told the story, and sent everyone home, the clock read almost midnight. He stuck his head in Rae's room to find Ben curled up beside her in the narrow hospital bed.

He opened his bleary eyes and gave Darren a half-smile. "I'll check on you tomorrow," Darren whispered before slipping out.

He called Farrah from his truck, but she didn't pick up. He knew she started early in the greenhouse, and instead of going all the way home, he went back to the Bybee's.

Neither Jim nor Corey was awake, but he tiptoed up

the stairs and collapsed into a bed in one of their spare bedrooms where he'd taken a Sunday afternoon nap before. His dreams were filled with red and blue police lights, tanks of tilapia, and the caramel-blonde hair of Farrah.

CHAPTER
TWELVE

Farrah could watch Darren sleep for hours. His handsomeness was only enhanced by the lack of cares, the unconsciousness of his mind. But Corey hadn't sent her up here to watch him sleep.

"Darren, wake up." She brushed her fingers across his forehead, his hair so close and calling to her so strongly. He'd called late last night, but she'd already been in bed. She wanted to tell him about the therapy session with her parents, which she'd thought had gone pretty great. He'd told her to call.

She'd been disappointed until she'd learned about Rae's accident. Then his behavior made sense. "Come on now," she whispered, leaning down. "You've gotta wake up. Corey's gonna—" She squealed as his arms snaked around her and pulled her onto the bed with him

"I'm tired," he moaned. "What time is it?"

"Almost eight, sleepyhead."

His eyes blinked open. "My mouth feels like I've swallowed a dead animal."

"And here I was gonna kiss you." She grinned as she pushed herself off the bed, away from him.

He stayed stock still, watching her. "I wouldn't do it," he said, though his eyes screamed at her that he wanted to kiss her badly. He pushed up on his elbows. "Will you come out to Steeple Ridge for dinner tonight? I'll cook."

Panic bolted through her like lightning. But she couldn't put him off forever. That was something Dr. Kenna had told her. *You have to make concessions too.*

Relationships are two way streets.

He needs something from you too, or he wouldn't still be with you.

And at the group therapy session last night, she'd confessed to everyone that she didn't like Steeple Ridge Farm, because that was where she'd learned the truth about who she was, and everyone in the room had disagreed with her.

Dr. Kenna said she learned the truth about who she was each day.

Her father had said she'd learned the truth about who she was when she rode a horse.

Her mother had said she'd learned the truth about who she was when she left LA and came home.

Farrah wasn't sure who was right. What she did know was that it meant a great deal to Darren that she go to Steeple Ridge.

"Yeah, sure," she said, trying for carefree and only halfway achieving it.

"Really?"

"Tell me what to bring."

He got to his feet and ran his hand through his hair. She wanted to do the same. "Just yourself, sweetheart. I'll even grill."

"Do you know how to use a grill? That's fire, you know." She folded her arms and grinned at him. So much in her life had improved over the past few weeks. Some because of him. Some because of what he'd challenged her to do. Some because of what he'd suggested she do.

She was talking to her parents again, and the therapy sessions helped more than she'd thought they would. Seeing him every day also brought a measure of peace and happiness to her life she'd been missing since May.

So overcome with gratitude and love for him, she stepped into his arms and hugged him tight. "How's Rae?"

"I don't know. Haven't heard anything this morning." He yawned and dipped his mouth to her throat. "I should get over to the hospital and then out to work. I'll call you later?" He tried to step away from her, but she held him in place.

He looked down at her with questions in his eyes.

"Tonight," she said, her gaze wandering to his mouth. She hadn't kissed him in months, had forgotten what he tasted like. But her cells knew what a strong mouth he had, how much tenderness he possessed in his lips, how safe and adored she felt when he kissed her.

"Tonight what?" he asked, his hands landing on her hips.

"Tonight, at the farm, after dinner...." She let her sentence hang there, sure by the way she was staring at his mouth that he'd be able to complete the sentence.

"You want ice cream?"

She giggled and looked up to see the teasing glint in his eyes. "No," she said. "I want you to kiss me."

He growled and pulled her closer. "Do we have to wait until tonight?"

"Yes."

He kissed her earlobe, rendering her weak and breathless. "Darren, you have to wait."

"I'm impatient," he whispered, his mouth migrating along her throat to her collarbone. "I don't think I can wait."

"You can."

"How are you so sure?" His breath mingled with hers, and if she'd had her eyes open she was sure she'd find his face only inches from hers.

"Because." She opened her eyes to his blinding good looks. "We're going to ride through the forest after dinner."

His eyebrows went up and his eyes widened, searching hers. "We are?"

"I believe that was the fantasy you described to me last week." She smiled. "You said you wanted to hold my hand while we rode out somewhere private. And then you wanted to kiss me."

"Did I say that? Are you sure I didn't say I wanted to kiss you in a spare bedroom at the Bybee's? Dreams change, you know."

"Farrah?" Corey called from downstairs. "Everything okay?"

Darren smiled wolfishly, his mouth dropping to her temple, then her eyelids, then her nose.

"Darren," she whispered.

"You don't have to come out to Steeple Ridge," he said. "We can ride here if you want. Jim will let us borrow his horses."

She shook her head as Corey called for her again. "Steeple Ridge. Tonight." He kissed her right cheek, then her left. "She's going to come up here, you know."

Darren pulled away just as the sound of footsteps came closer. "Steeple Ridge. Tonight." He moved away from her and said, "Mornin' Corey," before bending to swipe his cowboy hat from where it had fallen to the floor.

Farrah was left weak, hardly able to stand from the magical way he'd kissed her. And he hadn't even hit his target. Farrah shook her head at Corey, her hand lighting against the last place he'd kissed—the corner of her mouth —and a smile pulling against her resolve.

She moved to follow him into the hall and down the steps, but Corey blocked her way. "Farrah." She wrung her hands and she wore doe eyes. "I need you to be careful with him."

"Careful?"

"That man is in love with you, and he has been for months and months." Corey took a step closer and swallowed, her nerves clearly present but not preventing her from speaking. "When you broke up with him in May, it about killed him. I won't watch him suffer like that again."

That man is in love with you.

Farrah couldn't hear anything else. He'd said he'd fallen in love with her once. Could he still be in love with her now? Was that even possible after all she'd done, all she'd put him through?

Of course, she'd hoped for a second chance, and he'd been so willing to give it to her. But she hadn't expected him to fall in love with her so quickly.

"I won't hurt him," she promised Corey, who nodded, her bottom lip trembling the slightest bit. She backed out of the way, and Farrah stepped past her and hurried down to the botanical boutique.

That man is in love with you.

And for the first time in the last twelve years, Farrah felt like maybe, just maybe, she was lovable.

THAT EVENING, SHE TOOK GREAT CARE WITH HER CLOTHES, her jewelry, her makeup. She wanted everything to be perfect, romantic, for her second first kiss with Darren.

Her blouse billowed in the autumn wind, and she ran back inside to grab a jacket before leaving for the farm. She'd worn tight jeans and a pair of cowgirl boots she'd bought that very afternoon. She'd thrown away everything from her horseback riding life, an action she now regretted.

She pulled in at Steeple Ridge to find Darren sitting on the front porch, his hands between his knees. He'd obviously showered and changed into a fresh set of clothes too. She breathed in the spicy, sandalwoodsy scent of his cologne and skin before saying, "Hey, cowboy," in her best Southern drawl.

He grinned at her, that smile she'd craved every day since they'd broken up. "Hey, yourself. New boots?"

"Yep."

"Dinner's ready."

"Already?"

"It's getting dark earlier," he said, taking her hand and leading her into the farmhouse. This time, she didn't feel the insatiable need to glance around and remember everything that had happened here when she was a teenager. It had happened. It was done. Over.

"And I didn't want to cut our ride short. So dinner's ready." He stepped into the kitchen, bringing her with him. "Farrah, this is my farm family. Cody and Wade Caswell. Shiloh Davenport. Missy and Tucker Jenkins." He indicated each person as he said their name. She recognized everyone from church except for Shiloh.

"Guys, this is my girlfriend, Farrah Irvine."

Though she'd dated Darren for eight months before breaking things off with him, she'd never been out to the farm to officially meet his friends. His "farm family." They all shook her hand, and welcomed her, and then Tucker said a prayer for the safety and prosperity of the farm and all who worked it. He asked a blessing on the food, and they all moved outside, where the food had been laid out on a long picnic table to eat.

She learned that Shiloh had only been in town for a month, and that she wasn't particularly religious. She learned that Wade liked to speak less than Darren did. She learned that Cody had an affinity for dogs the same way Logan had. And she learned that Missy and Tucker had just bought four more horses for next summer's riding camp.

Finally, Darren stood from the backyard picnic table and said, "We'll catch up with y'all later." He tucked her hand in his as they strolled toward the barn. The sky was starting to bruise, and she hurried to saddle the horse he'd given her, a beautiful dark chocolate-colored horse named Mint Brownie.

She swung easily into the saddle, the feel of it against her legs absolutely right. She basked in the evening sunshine as she and Darren steered their steeds toward the tree line beyond the pastures.

He reached over and took her hand. "You're a beautiful rider," he said.

"I miss it," she confessed.

"Yeah?"

She nodded, a smile forming on her face as she realized she'd been depriving herself of things she loved for a long time. And why? Because she didn't think they were emblems of her authentic self. Because she hadn't known who she was.

She still didn't have all of the pieces, but she had several. "I like horseback riding," she said, more to herself than to Darren.

They rode in companionable silence until Darren pointed up ahead. "There's the clearing where we usually stop for lunch."

"You ride out here everyday?"

"I wish." He chuckled. "Just sometimes. If we're working in the pastures or the fence lines. Then we pack lunches and eat out here. It's peaceful."

That it was. She swung off Mint Brownie and tossed his reins over the same branch Darren did. The two horses began to graze on the tall forest grasses, and Darren spread a blanket on the ground. "If we sit here, we can watch the sun set right over that hill." He sat and then moved to the left a few inches before patting the blanket for her to join him.

She did, curling into the warmth of his embrace. "Dinner was great," she said.

He breathed in deep and then released it. "I can't lie; Missy made most of it."

Farrah startled and pulled back to look at him. "You didn't cook me dinner?"

"I set the table. Does that count?"

"No, it does not." Farrah giggled and cuddled in closer. "It's fine. It was grilled chicken and asparagus."

"And balsamic glaze. Tucker made that."

Farrah shook her head. "Why didn't you make it?"

"I was too busy freaking out. They took pity on me."

"Freaking out? About what?"

He waved his hand toward the horizon. "This. You coming to the farm. Rae. Sam. All of it."

"What's wrong with Sam?"

"Nothing. He's great."

She waited for him to say more, but he didn't. "Darren."

"I just miss him," he said. "He was like my dad for a

while, and I've just had some experiences that have reminded me to be grateful for what he did when our parents died." He cut her a glance out of the corner of his eye. "That's all."

She watched the sun dip lower in the sky. "Will we be able to get back in the dark?"

"We'll leave as soon as the sun goes down," he said. "There will still be enough light to get back."

Several more seconds passed before Darren shifted beside her. She glanced up at him, and he stroked his fingers down the side of her face. "Farrah, I know it's crazy, and probably way too soon to tell you this, but I think I'm in love with you again."

She blinked, unsure of how to respond. So she tilted her head back and received his kiss willingly, sparks shooting through her whole body at the contact.

She'd kissed Darren before—lots of times—but this kiss definitely held something more. He really did love her. She basked in the warmth of it, let it send shockwaves through her muscles, and deepened the kiss so he would know she might be in love with him too.

CHAPTER
THIRTEEN

Nothing existed when Darren kissed Farrah. The sky could fall, the sun could burn to dust, everything could disappear from existence.

He marveled at the way she kissed him, like she really enjoyed herself and couldn't get enough of him. Which was perfect, because he absolutely couldn't kiss her for long enough. He laid her down on the blanket and kissed her again and again, almost like he'd been starving without her touch these past few months.

He finally remembered his manners and pulled away. She tucked herself against his chest and they watched the sun sink lower and lower in the sky.

He couldn't believe he'd confessed that he loved her. But he wanted to tell her, wanted her to know the depth of his feelings now, so she wouldn't run away later.

And she hadn't run. She'd stayed. Stayed and kissed him.

His heart beat erratically in his chest, rejoicing to be here with her, playing out one of his fantasies. The gentle rise in the landscape finally swallowed the sun, and he said, "Well, we should go."

She groaned and held onto him as he tried to stand. "One more kiss."

He chuckled and planted his lips against her forehead.

"No," she complained. "That wasn't a good kiss."

"You're saying I'm not a good kisser?"

She gazed up at him with those blue eyes, so full of trust and hope and…love? "Better prove it," she whispered in the semi-darkness.

He touched his lips to hers for just a beat, barely there then gone. A tingle started against his tongue, and he kissed her again, holding on longer and really exploring her mouth. She responded in kind, and he knew without a shadow of a doubt that he would never be satisfied kissing anyone else.

"All right," he said a bit breathlessly. "We really do have to get back." They got up and he folded the blanket and stowed it back in the saddlebag. They arrived back at Steeple Ridge with only a hint of light left in the sky.

Working beside her to brush down the horses was almost as exciting as kissing her, and Darren couldn't help glancing over at her every few seconds. She seemed to be watching him just as much, because as soon as they put away the animals, she grabbed onto his shirt collar and pressed him into the stall door for another kiss.

He wanted to kiss her everywhere. Here. In the other barn. Giggling as they ducked around the corner of the shed to steal a kiss. In the house. Next to her car. He simply couldn't get enough of her.

"Lunch tomorrow?" she said against his lips. "The forest is only a few steps from the boutique."

He nipped her bottom lip and claimed her mouth again. "I'll be there."

She ducked her head and tucked her hair behind her ears. "Darren, I'm sorry about—"

"Not tonight, Farrah." He placed one finger on her lips and stroked it across them. "We're fine. Nothing to be sorry about."

She looked like she wanted to argue, but she didn't. Darren went with her to her car and he got that kiss next to it before she climbed in and drove down the lane back to the highway. He watched her headlights until they disappeared, his hands stuck low in his pockets. He gazed up into the dark sky, where the stars had just started to wink into existence.

"Thank you, Lord," he said. "For bringing her home to Steeple Ridge." For bringing her home to *him*.

DARREN SNUCK AWAY FOR LUNCH WHEN HE SHOULD'VE BEEN prepping a field for mowing. He reasoned that he wouldn't be on the tractor until tomorrow, and he could check the fences after dinner. But he absolutely couldn't miss lunch.

He arrived at the Bybee's farm and parked next to Farrah's car near the house. The botanical boutique sat down a dirt path and into the hillside as it dipped toward the forest. The fish tank had been partially built underground, which made it easier to maintain the temperature.

Farrah pushed out of the greenhouse just as he was about to reach for the door handle. "Oh." She startled, recognized him, and giggled all in a second's time. In the next moment, she jerked her head toward the trees to the right of the building. "I usually eat out here."

With his heart pounding, he held up his paper bag, which contained a hastily put together peanut butter sandwich and a half a bag of potato chips that belonged to Wade. Darren would need to replace them before the other cowboy discovered they were gone or face dire consequences.

Farrah spoke about her work in the greenhouse, and how much better it was than the bowling alley. Darren nodded and smiled, glad she liked her job more now than she had only a few weeks ago.

"You're quiet today," she said.

He swallowed the last bite of his sandwich. "I like listening to you talk."

She ducked her head, causing her hair to fall between them like a glorious blonde curtain. He resisted the urge to brush it back, curl his fingers around the back of her neck, and draw her mouth to his.

He didn't want to come on too strong, didn't want to make the first move this time. She inched toward him, snuggling in close to his side. "Tell me something about Steeple Ridge."

"You know all about that place." He didn't want to talk

about the farm she could barely tolerate. Although, she had seemed perfectly at ease with him at the farm the previous day. She'd laughed during dinner, made pleasant conversation, and the horseback ride had been easy and carefree.

"I know about it from twelve years ago. It's changed."

Darren gazed through the trees, the blue sky peeking through the leaves. "I love Steeple Ridge." He sighed. "It's the first farm that has ever felt like home."

"You've worked at a lot of farms?"

"Yes." Darren hadn't told her much of his history before Steeple Ridge, mostly because he couldn't get her to talk about the farm at all. He'd told her about his parents' farm in Coral Canyon, where Sam had gone, and about their deaths. But not much of what had happened in between then and now. "Vermont is my favorite state."

"So you're going to stay here?"

He glanced down at her, but he couldn't meet her eyes. "Yeah." Was she not going to stay here? What kind of question was that? "Are you?"

She exhaled and leaned her weight into him, causing him to fall back slightly. He gave in to gravity and laid back into the soft grass, taking Farrah with him. She laid her head against his chest, nearly over his heart. "I'm going to stay here, especially now that I have this job." She twitched against his side. "I have thought about going back to school and finishing my agribusiness degree."

"Yeah?"

"Yeah, I could go to the University of Vermont in Burlington. It's only a half-hour drive."

"And your parents live there."

"Right." But she didn't seem overly enthused about stopping by to visit her parents after her college classes.

"You should do that, if you want," he said. "I was never much for college."

"No?"

"Not much of a reader."

"You could do ranch management or something."

"Pretty sure a farm and a ranch are two different things."

Farrah pushed up on her elbow and supported her head with her hand as she gazed down at him. "Did you want to go to college, and you just couldn't—because of your parents?" She trailed her free fingers across his chest, stirring something deep inside him.

He shook his head without looking away from her. "No. I wouldn't have gone. Logan wanted to though."

"And now he is."

Darren couldn't help reaching up and tucking those errant curls. "You seem like you'd be a good fit for college."

"Meagan told me she wants to quit when she has her baby." Farrah lifted her shoulder in a sexy shrug. "I think the Bybees would hire me full-time, with benefits, in her place."

"I'm sure they would." A slip of joy pulled through him at the thought of her becoming permanent at this farm. At her having a life she wanted.

"Darren, I have to tell you something." She leaned over and skated her lips along his jaw. His eyes drifted closed but his senses remained on high alert. Instead of telling him anything with words, she touched her lips to his. That was all the encouragement Darren needed, and he tangled his legs with hers as he kissed her and kissed her.

After several minutes, she said, "Darren." She giggled and tried to pull away.

He kept her right where he wanted her easily. "Mm."

"Your hip is vibrating."

"They'll call back."

"They've called twice."

Reluctantly, Darren turned onto his back. His mouth felt bruised and his head too hot. Still, his phone vibrated in his pocket. He pulled it out and saw Logan's name on the screen. "It's Logan." He swiped on the call. "Do you mind?"

Farrah sat up and ran her hands through her hair. "Of course not."

"Logan, hey." Darren exhaled as he sat up too. "What's goin' on? How's California?"

Farrah got up and strolled away, casting a flirty *follow-me-if-you-dare* look at Darren. He wanted to hang up with his brother and go wherever she did.

"I heard a rumor," his brother said in a playful, teasing voice. "That you got back together with Farrah Irvine."

Darren rolled his eyes and kept his sigh contained. "Who called you? Tucker? Missy?"

"Ben."

Of course. Ben, who just wanted everyone to be as happy as he was. The youngest brother who never caused any problems. The perpetual peacemaker. "Did he tell you about Rae's accident?"

"Yes. Said she's doing a lot better now."

"She is."

"Don't change the subject," Logan said, chuckling. "I thought Farrah wouldn't talk to you after you submitted her name for the parade."

Darren really needed to call his brother more often. The thought of starting at the beginning of the story made his stomach tighten. "I'm with Farrah right now," he said. "Can I call you later?"

"Ooh, did I interrupt you?" Logan laughed now. "You're kissing her again, aren't you?"

"Logan." Darren tried to put on his best big-brother warning voice, though he was only older by a few minutes.

"Do you think that's wise?"

"What?"

"Darren."

"Logan."

"I'm worried you'll get your heart broken again."

Darren was worried about that too, though when he kissed Farrah and felt the passion and adoration in her touch, those fears disappeared. "Better than what I was doin', Logan." Darren spoke very low, but very clear.

Logan sighed, and his brotherly concern traveled all the way across the country. "I'm sorry, Darren." He meant he was sorry for leaving Vermont, though he was coming back. He meant he was sorry all the other brothers had started dating before Darren. He meant a lot more than just that Darren had suffered for a few months without Farrah at his side.

Darren got to his feet and tried to find Farrah, who'd slunk deeper into the woods. He said the same thing to Logan as he'd said to Farrah. "Nothing to be sorry about, Logan. I have to go."

"You better call me every other day!" Logan called as if Darren would hang up on him. "I want details of this relationship."

"Me too!" a woman called, and it had to be Layla, Logan's wife.

"Layla does too, and she also says she's really excited for you and Farrah."

Darren chuckled, though he didn't quite understand why Layla was excited for him. "Tell her hello," he said just as Farrah turned and lifted her eyebrows as if to say *Well? Are you coming?*

"I really need to go." He hung up without saying goodbye to his twin. He tossed the phone onto the brown paper bag he'd brought his lunch in and strode after Farrah. Her giggles reached his ears, and he hurried to find her in the maze of pines and basswoods.

When he did, she kissed him so completely that he didn't worry any longer about his heart staying whole.

Because she kissed him like she loved him.

CHAPTER
FOURTEEN

Farrah was in deep with Darren, and she knew it. So deep she really had to stop kissing him and start talking. But kissing was so much more fun, and safe, and she was desperate to keep him in her life.

And if he knew certain things, she wasn't sure he'd stick around. Although the way he kissed her, held her tightly and softly at the same time, maybe he would.

"I have to go." He ducked his head, his breathing ragged. "I have to get the fields ready for mowing tomorrow."

She nodded and bit her lip. She had work to do as well, and if he left, she'd have a few more hours where she could call him her boyfriend.

"What did you want to tell me?" He lifted his gaze to look right into hers, piercing her with those dark eyes, that even temper.

"Oh, it's—" She couldn't bring herself to say "nothing." Because it was something. At least she thought it was.

He waited, his patience seemingly endless. She knew that wasn't true, and when the muscle in his jaw started twitching, she knew he was working hard to keep waiting.

She'd imagined this moment since the second she'd started dating him, almost a year ago now. He already knew her last name was different, and the rumors around town were that she'd been married and divorced.

They were sort of right, and Farrah had done nothing to correct them.

"I—" She swallowed, the ham and cheese sandwich she'd eaten for lunch threatening to come back up. Farrah stepped back to get some air that wasn't filled with the hay-scented quality of his skin, the touch of sunshine he infused into her life.

"When I lived in California, I dated a man named Garrett Irvine."

Darren settled his weight on his back foot and shoved his hands in his pocket, the picture of sexiest cowboy alive. "Ah, so there's the Irvine. You got married?"

Why he asked like he couldn't believe it, she wasn't sure. She shook her head, the ends of her hair brushing her forearms. "We didn't actually get married. I was—" She pressed her eyes closed. "I got pregnant, and I didn't want to have the baby alone, so I told everyone we were married."

She heard him suck in a breath, but she wasn't brave enough to open her eyes and look at him.

"I've seen your driver's license," he said. "It says Farrah Irvine."

"I legally changed it after he—after we ended things. He didn't know about the baby at the time, but when he found out, he wanted me to end the pregnancy." Her vision began to spin, and she had to open her eyes so she wouldn't fall down.

She hadn't explained things very well, but Darren didn't usually need long explanations. Garrett had broken up with her before she'd discovered she was pregnant. When she told him, he'd texted back to say *Well, then take care of it.*

And he didn't mean have the baby and mother it.

She couldn't—*wouldn't*—do anything to hurt the child, so she'd changed her name, moved to a new apartment, and started telling people her husband was overseas serving in the military. The number of lies she'd told swallowed her whole, even now, and she couldn't believe she'd come back to the light from such a place of darkness.

Darren's fingertips brushed her forearm. "So you were never married."

She focused on the skin he'd touched. "No."

"But you told people you were."

"Yes."

"And you changed your name."

"Yes."

"And you had a baby."

She shook her head, her bottom lip trembling along with the motion. "No."

He slid two fingers under her chin and lifted her face so she'd look at him. "No?"

"I was pregnant for eighty-nine days. I lost the baby."

He wrapped his arms around her without another word, and she let him comfort her for something that had happened four years ago. How the pain was still there seemed ridiculous, especially because she had never felt so lost, so isolated, so utterly forgotten by God, than she had in that period of her life.

"After that," she whispered into his shirt. "I started coming back to church. I met a pastor in Los Angeles that helped me for two solid years to rebuild my faith and find my way through the repentance process."

Darren said nothing. Most of the time she didn't need him to. Now, though, she wanted to hear him whisper that everything was okay, that she was fine, that he still loved her.

The moment lengthened, and all of Farrah's memories streamed through her mind. She'd kept them boxed up, vowing never to let them out. But she hadn't anticipated meeting someone as wonderful as Darren. Honestly, she hadn't planned on dating anyone ever again.

And maybe that's why you broke up with him over a parade. The thought sprang into her mind, unbidden but there nonetheless. Maybe it was. Everything about Darren scared her, and though she liked being with him, she wasn't sure she could ever be comfortable with him.

Now that she'd confessed a few of her secrets to him, it was easier to be with him. She just couldn't believe he still *wanted* to be with her.

He cleared his throat. "I really do have to go."

She stepped back and nodded, a tear threatening to escape. She wasn't even sure why. He hadn't broken up with her. He hadn't condemned her. But he was walking away from her, and he didn't look back.

She almost called after him to come to her place for dinner, but if she'd been told that the man she loved had almost had a child with someone he wasn't married to, she'd need some time to process. And while Darren hadn't usually needed much time to know what he wanted, she suspected that this time he would.

BY THE WEEKEND, FARRAH HAD SPOKEN ON THE PHONE WITH Darren a couple of times, but he wasn't a great conversationalist, so she'd resorted back to texting. He seemed to do that just fine, mostly because he rarely responded immediately. He was overthinking things, and she suspected that he was typing and re-typing his responses before sending them.

Friday night—date night—came, and Farrah did not have a date. "What are you doing tonight?" she asked Meagan, more to make conversation than anything else.

"Bunko night," she said, glancing up from the raft where she worked. She did a double-take before straightening. She scanned Farrah from head to toe. "Do you play? Because Hannah texted about an hour ago and said she's sick and can't come. We need another player."

"I've never played bunko."

"It's my month to host, so it's at my place." Meagan rushed toward her. "It's so easy, and there's dinner provided, and I'll even pay your five dollars for the prize pot." Her eyes lit up, and Farrah couldn't help laughing.

"I don't have any plans," she said, and Meagan engulfed her in a hug, her tiny baby bump solid against Farrah's stomach. She sobered quickly then and stepped back. "So what time?"

"Six. Don't eat before. There's tons of food and Rae brings her mother's secret recipe almond punch every month. This month's theme is the fall harvest, and I've been baking with pumpkin and apples and maple syrup all week."

Farrah was sure she'd just gotten in way over her head, but she thought anything was better than sitting home alone on a Friday night. "Is there usually a monthly theme?"

"Oh, yeah," Meagan said. "Hannah did a whole maple syrup shindig in April, and before Layla moved—wow. She'd plan her month perfectly, and it was the best party of the year." She sighed wistfully. "Rae always has good food, because she caters from La Ferrovia." Meagan grinned. "I'm so glad you're joining us. You'll love it."

Farrah wasn't so sure of that. She'd avoided spending time with the women in LA, because no one could be trusted. Everyone was out for themselves.

You're not in LA anymore, she told herself as she went back to planting cilantro seeds. *And maybe it's time you started making more friends in Island Park.* She'd probably know every woman there, especially if they were

Meagan's friends. As they finished work, and Farrah headed home, she decided that having some friends in town wouldn't be such a bad idea.

She spent an hour in her yard in the cooling fall temperatures, watching the clock on her phone tick closer and closer to six. She wasn't sure if bunko was the type of party one could show up fashionably late for, so she fed Bolt, showered quickly, and tied her damp hair into a knot on the top of her head before slipping into a casual pair of khaki capris and a blouse the color of watermelon rinds.

When she arrived at Meagan's, it was clear she should've come earlier. The door opened to a wall of sound, from music, to chatter, to laughter, to a dog barking somewhere beyond the party. It seemed like fifty women had packed themselves inside her living room and kitchen, but upon further inspection, Farrah counted eleven others besides herself.

Three tables filled the area, with colorful signs on red, brown, and white plaid paper that said *high*, *medium*, and *low*. She had no idea what they meant but instinctively hoped she wouldn't be put at the low table.

"Come in, come in." Meagan grinned at her like she was the Queen of England. "Guys, Farrah's here."

Every eye turned toward her, and sure enough, Farrah recognized almost every face. Missy and Rae were the friendliest, and they came over to her. Rae had recovered decently well from her car accident, and she wore a full leg brace as she hobbled closer. "Look at you." She grinned and glanced at Missy. "I didn't think this was your scene."

The scent of freshly baked pie crust filled the air, along

with something sweet and cidery. With this many women, and this much noise, Farrah could easily say, "Oh, it's not. But Meagan needed a sub, and well." She shrugged, not wanting to admit she didn't have anything else to do that night.

"Glad you came." Missy gave her shoulders a squeeze and turned back to the crowd. "Okay, so you have to watch out for April. She works at the rec center with Rae, and they cannot be partners."

"It's a game of chance," Rae said, a note of defensiveness in her tone.

"Still." Missy gave her a look that spoke of how much time they'd spent together. "They're like a luck charm when they're on the same team."

"There's teams?" Farrah asked, letting herself get swept toward the crowd.

"You'll be partnered with someone different in every game," Missy said. "You know Logan's wife? Well, Aria and Hazel still work at Layla's clinic."

Farrah said hello to them, glad for another connection between her and a couple of the women.

"You know Audra and Meagan from the farm," Missy continued. "And Meredith works at the rec too. Michelle and Cheryl—" Two women turned, punch cups in hand and wide smiles on their faces. "Work at the elementary school. They're friends of Bonnie's." Missy gestured to Farrah. "She's dating Darren Buttars."

The way she said it so casually made Farrah's insides dance. The way Michelle and Cheryl's faces lit up, as if they had nothing but mad respect for Darren, helped Farrah feel more at ease.

"And this is Toby," Missy said, indicating the last woman. She sported bleached hair no longer than an inch. "She runs the yoga studio by the bookstore, and I think…Meredith goes there." She raised her eyebrows and looked at Toby.

"That's right." She smiled and shook Farrah's hand. Out of all of the women, Toby hadn't grown up here in Island Park, and Farrah found herself wanting to be her partner.

A cowbell rang, nearly deafening Farrah, and she spun to find Meagan holding it gleefully. "Come get your scorecards and pencils," she announced into the resulting silence. "And game one begins in sixty seconds!"

Panic flooded Farrah. "I don't know how to play," she blurted, hoping one of the women making a mad dash for the scorecards and pencils would stop and teach her. They didn't.

Missy returned and handed her a card with a big blue M in the corner. "You're at the medium table, and it looks like there's only one spot left. You'll be Aria's partner."

Aria, Aria. Farrah had met so many women in such a short time, but she managed to locate the medium table and the woman sitting across from the open space. Farrah took her scorecard and pencil and headed over.

She sat and smiled at Aria, who grinned back. "I've never played," she said. "I'm so sorry."

Aria tipped her head back and laughed. She waved her hand. "Honey, it's rolling dice. You can handle it."

"Can she?" Michelle asked. "Because Audra and I were a team last month, and we killed it." She high-fived Audra across the table.

Farrah blinked, completely unprepared for smack talk from grown women at bunko night. A smile spread her lips. Oh, this *was* going to be fun.

CHAPTER
FIFTEEN

Darren stood in the cemetery, feeling like he was doing something wrong. He glanced around again, satisfied that no one else was there. He stared down at the headstone Farrah had been looking at a few months ago.

Gary Karl Lewis.

No Irvine in sight. So not her—not the father of her baby. Not her baby either. No, this man was sixty-four-years-old, and Darren's need to know who he was a sixty-four out of ten.

He turned away from the headstone and strode over to Paintbrush. The horse snacked on the grass under a tree, and Darren led him out of the shade. One more furtive glance around, and he swung up onto the horse's back.

"Let's get out of here," he muttered.

It had been days since Farrah had told him about part of her time in LA. She had such a big heart, and had always been so honest with him, that finding out about a completely different side of her had been shocking.

He'd spoken with her a few times, and texted lots more. But she'd been silent since yesterday afternoon, and when he'd called Logan on a Friday night, his brother's first question had been, "Why aren't you out with Farrah?"

That had sent Darren into a tailspin. He'd gone by her house, the way he used to do when he was crushing on a girl in high school. Maybe not exactly like that. He and Logan hadn't seemed to ever have a problem getting dates. Logan was a real charmer, and girls found Darren's quiet, mysterious demeanor intriguing. Usually. *Teenage* girls had.

But Farrah's house had been dark. Her car gone.

She'd been out on a Friday night, and he'd been too much of a chicken to text her and find out where she was.

He took his time riding back to the farm, gave Paintbrush the royal treatment in horse care, and made sure all the weekend chores were done before he went into the farmhouse. The country stillness extended into the house, and Darren breathed in the peacefulness of it.

Showered and ready for a date, he called Farrah, praying she'd answer. When she did, her voice sounded guarded. Maybe. Maybe just rushed. He wasn't sure.

"I was hopin' you didn't have plans tonight," he said. "And that maybe we could…do something."

"Oh." She exhaled, and he could just see her thinking, that adorable line that appeared between her eyes when she did. "I've been in the yard all day, and I'm a mess."

"I'm not in a hurry."

"What did you have in mind?"

"Anything but a crowd."

She giggled. "You would've died at bunko night."

Confusion pulled through him. He stepped over to the fridge and opened it. "I'm sorry. What's bunko night?"

"Meagan invited me, and I went last night. You would not believe the noise. Crashing dice, and screeching ladies, and trash talk."

"Trash talk?" Darren paused in lifting a water bottle to his lips. "What did you say?"

"Nothing, I swear." She laughed fully now, and he wished he was with her so he could bask in her happiness. "But I had a great time. Meagan says if someone drops out next year, I can have the spot."

"You'll have to tell me what that means when I come over." He started drinking, his eyes landing on the keys hanging on the hook nearby. He swallowed. "When can I come over?"

"I'll go jump in the shower right now."

"Great, see you in a few." Darren hung up, thinking he could just drive slow. Maybe entertain her cat while she did whatever she did with her makeup to enhance her natural beauty.

He arrived at her house, the evidence of her green thumb in the trimmed lawn, the newly barked flowerbeds, the pruned bushes and trees. Bolt, her gray tabby, sat on top of the front steps like a guard.

Darren eyed him as he parked and got out of the truck. "Hey, kitty cat."

The cat just stared, not even a twitch of the tail. It was

no wonder Darren liked dogs better. He went past the animal and knocked on the door. Farrah opened it a few moments later, her hair still damp. The fruity-soft scent of her conditioner drifted into his nose, and he leaned against the doorjamb.

"The yard looks amazing."

"Getting ready for winter," she said. "It can come fast here."

"Yeah." Darren couldn't seem to look away from her. She hadn't put her makeup on yet, but she didn't need it. He wanted to apologize for his days of silence. For his Friday night blunder. He reached for her, slipping his hand around the back of her neck, right into that silky hair, and bringing her mouth to his.

His kiss was filled with apology and hers with acceptance. He ended the union sooner than he would've liked and leaned his forehead against hers. "So I was thinking we could grab something to go and go out to the Bybee's. Or the lake."

"Lake," she whispered. "I spend all day at that farm."

Of course she did. Darren hadn't been out there since she'd told him about her non-husband—whose name she still used—and he missed the tranquility of it. But the lake would do.

Darren loved Lake Champlain late in the year, and he'd spent some time on it the first winter all the brothers lived in Vermont. Sam was a fan of ice fishing, and Darren was the only one who would go with him. He hadn't been since his brother had gone back to Wyoming, at least not in the winter.

He'd been back a few times in the warmer months, but he didn't enjoy boating or lying in the sun, and he had too much work to do besides. But a picnic dinner on the beach sounded pretty great.

"Let me change," she said. "It's not exactly warm once the sun goes down."

"We can sit in the truck," he offered as she backed away from him.

"I'll just put on jeans and grab a jacket."

Darren mourned the loss of her denim shorts, but he liked the dark jeans she showed up wearing as well. She opened her front closet and plucked a sweatshirt from a hanger before saying, "Ready."

"What do you want to eat?"

"Let's get sandwiches from the Bread Company."

Darren never said no to a sandwich, and a half an hour later, they had food, drinks, and the sand between their toes.

"Your feet are so white." She laughed as she handed him his sandwich.

"Always wearing boots." He chuckled with her. "So tell me about this bunko night."

She started talking, and he liked listening to her. She told him about a dice game, and baby bunkos, and a prize pool, and several women from her childhood that she'd played with.

"Sounds like you had fun."

"I really did," she said, smiling before she bit into her sandwich. "I hate to say it, but I hope someone drops out so I can join permanently."

"You can't just join?"

"The group only handles twelve." She gazed at the gently lapping water. "Each person takes a month to host. The host provides dinner, and the previous month's host provides the prizes." She sighed, a happy little sound Darren liked. "I won for the most baby bunkos, and I got a certificate to the salon for a pedicure."

"That's great," he said. "I guess I hope someone drops out so you can join."

"I don't think someone will." This time her sigh carried a bit more weight. "They all get along great, and they've been a bunko group for three years."

"No one's left in three years?" Darren was still getting used to the idea of not moving every few years.

"Well, Layla left, but she's coming back. The person they got to take her place knows it's only until she returns."

Darren nestled his toes deeper into the sand. A breeze wafted across the water, and he watched a few sailboats bump against the waves as they worked against their anchors. The deep green trees stretched into the blue sky, and the hills across the lake were quickly turning black against the horizon.

In the winter, the ice on those trees would break limbs, and in a week or two, the leaves would be various shades of red, gold, and orange.

"I love Vermont," Farrah said, breaking the silence that had come between them.

"Better than LA?" he asked.

"The beaches were nice," she said. "And it doesn't

snow there. But there's just something about this place." She snuggled into his side, sticking her arms through her sweatshirt without pulling it over her head.

He knew exactly what she meant, and he was glad she liked it here. "Want to go riding tomorrow after church?"

She stiffened next to him, and all the things Darren had been careful not to say came rushing to the front of his mind.

"Farrah, when are you going to stop fighting against who you are?"

She sat up and looked at him, her gaze sharp. "What does that mean?"

"You were born to ride a horse," he said. "And it doesn't matter who you were born from."

She blinked. Her jaw tightened. He thought sure she'd jump to her feet and stomp back to the truck.

"It's just me," he said. "Me and you, out riding through the fields and forests. I know you like it. I *know* you do."

Her chin trembled. "I do like it."

He tucked her against his side again. "Why is that so hard to admit?"

"I'm still…learning a lot about myself."

"So you'll come riding?"

She nudged him with her shoulder. "You're relentless."

"Thank you."

"That wasn't a compliment." She giggled.

He growled and dipped his head toward hers. "I thought it was." Skating his lips along her neck, he asked, "Who's Gary Lewis?"

She did jump to her feet this time. Just enough sun

remained for him to see her absolute fury. "I told you not to worry about him," she said.

"No." He stood too. "You told me not to look him up. I didn't." He reached for her, and she let him take one of her hands in his. But he was breaths away from losing her, and he knew it. "I just want to know who he is."

"So do I."

He watched her, trying to figure out what she meant. "You don't know who he is?"

"I know who he is, but not who he was as a person." Tears turned her eyes bright and glassy.

"Farrah," Darren said in his gentlest voice. "I just want to help you. Know everything about you. That's what people do, you know."

He watched something inside her break, and he hated it. Hated the way those tears spilled out of her lovely eyes. "He was my father," she said. "And he didn't want me." She collapsed into his arms, and Darren held her close to his heart while she cried.

CHAPTER
SIXTEEN

Farrah couldn't believe how much liquid came out of her face. Everything felt too hot though the sun had gone behind the hills several minutes ago.

Darren kept his strong arms around her, creating an eye in the storm of her emotions. She felt safe with him, but she didn't elaborate. She'd have to eventually, but maybe he'd be satisfied with what she'd already told him. After all, she hadn't told anyone the story of meeting her birth father, because it pierced her deep and bit hard.

"Should we go?" he whispered.

She nodded, still sniffling, and allowed him to sweep up their trash and the blanket he'd spread on the sand before tucking her hand in his and leading her up the beach to the parking lot. She'd loved this beach growing up. It had tall trees growing right out of the sand, and she had happy memories of making sandcastles and burying her father up to his neck.

Doesn't matter that Gary didn't want you, she told herself. *You have parents.*

She needed to talk to Dr. Kenna, but her next appointment wasn't until Tuesday. She seriously considered calling the therapist, but then Darren leaned into the truck, reaching across her to buckle her seatbelt. "There you go." He gazed at her with such love, she decided right then that she didn't need the love or acceptance of the father who had donated his sperm to her existence.

She trailed her fingers down the side of his face. "I'm scared you're going to grow weary of me," she said. "I came home with a lot of baggage."

He gazed back at her evenly, not so much as a twitch or a blink. "We can unpack it one thing at a time."

One thing at a time.

Dr. Kenna had said something similar. She'd counseled Farrah not to try to tackle everything at once. And she hadn't. But she felt like she was juggling a lot of balls. Her job. Her new relationship with her parents. Her past. Her memories. New friends. Darren.

No matter what, she couldn't drop Darren. His ball seemed made of glass, and she was sure she didn't have many more chances with him. If she dropped his ball, it would shatter, and she simply couldn't afford to lose him.

She nodded, her heart swelling with love for him. He walked around the front of the truck and got behind the wheel. "Maybe we can watch a movie at your place."

"You've seen all my movies."

He started the truck and adjusted the heater. "Want to go to the theater in Burlington?"

She shook her head. "What have you got at the farmhouse?"

He swung toward her, his surprise easy to see through the dimming light. "You want to come out to Steeple Ridge and watch a movie at my house?"

"Will the other cowboys mind?"

"I don't care if they do."

A smile spread her lips. "Darren."

"I don't know what Cody and Wade are doin'. And Shiloh moved in too."

"We could get a movie and take it to my house."

He backed out of the parking space. "No, let's go see what's going on at Steeple Ridge." He drove away from the lake, the Adirondack Mountains black now against the navy blue sky. She felt spent, so tired her brain seemed to be sloshing from one side of her skull to the other. But she didn't want to be alone, and as Darren drove through the old town feel of Island Park and along the winding highway to Steeple Ridge, she felt like she was going home.

Lights shone in the farmhouse windows, and a memory surged forward. She'd come out to Steeple Ridge after a fight with her mother, the homey feel of the farmhouse a welcome beacon in that dark night.

Jamie had received her with concern, even though she'd already gone to bed. She'd made chocolate milk from powder and pulled out her secret stash of gingerbread cookies. She'd let Farrah cry, and she hadn't asked a single question.

In the end, she'd told her she needed to go home and

make things right with her mother.

"When things went bad in Los Angeles, I thought about Steeple Ridge." She spoke to the darkness beyond her window.

Darren put the truck in park but didn't get out. "Oh?"

"Jamie, the woman who used to own the farm before Tucker, was like a second mother to me. She was my riding instructor, and she taught me a lot more than how to jump and care for horses."

Darren said nothing, and Farrah found she didn't need him to. She could feel his attentiveness, and it was one of his most attractive qualities. That, and his dark, delicious eyes.

"Did you ever know Jamie?"

"I'm afraid not," he said so quietly she could barely hear him.

Farrah sighed, her breath fogging the window the slightest bit. "She was great. She made Steeple Ridge feel like home, and she helped me through some hard times when I was a teenager and didn't get along with my mom."

Darren shifted on the seat. "I'm glad."

"Yeah, she told me once that I needed to go home and make things right. So when I lost everything in LA, I thought of what she said. It was almost like she was there, whispering in my ear. Leading me. Guiding me. And I came home."

But not to Steeple Ridge. She'd been back in Island Park for over a year before she'd come out to this farm, and even then, she'd only come under duress. She wasn't sure why she thought she needed to abandon everything she'd been before leaving Vermont. She realized now that her childhood was part of her—a vital part—and that just because she had stranger's blood flowing in her veins that didn't mean she was different.

"I'm glad you came home," he said. And he genuinely sounded like he was.

"I tracked my dad down in California. That's why I went there." Her voice sounded somewhat alien, almost like she'd lost control of herself. "He was a producer, but he didn't want me in any of his productions." Her chest pinched. Her throat narrowed. "He asked me a lot of questions about my life and myself. But he didn't really care. In the end, he asked me to leave and never come back."

"He's why you left LA?"

"No. Yes. Not really." She finally turned toward Darren, whose cowboy hat kept his face bathed in darkness. "He just meant not to contact him again. I was so...." Angry. Scared. Devastated.

She cleared her throat. "It was a hard time. I decided to leave LA because I wasn't happy there. All I could think about was Steeple Ridge." Her gaze drifted back to the farmhouse, where a dog waited with his tongue panting out of his mouth.

Steeple Ridge, with its dogs and horses. Miles of pastures. Green rolling hills and bright blue skies. A cheery farmhouse with yellow lights shining in the windows. She'd held this idyllic picture of the farm in her mind, and she hadn't wanted to ruin it by coming back and seeing that it had changed.

But the spirit of the farm hadn't changed. The charm and magic of it remained, even if Tucker had painted the house a brighter white and Missy had expanded the show arena.

"A few days after I got here," Farrah continued. "Someone called to tell me my father had died, and he had no one. No family. Nowhere to be buried. No will. Nothing. So I brought him here. I had my original birth certificate, and I got his estate."

She didn't want it. Had asked her lawyer to sell everything he could and manage the bank account. Movement to her right caught her attention, and she saw Cody leading a horse toward the barn.

"I have a lot of money," she said, turning toward Darren again. "I want to buy some horses with it." She felt shaky and weak, and she hated that. "I want to ride horses again."

He reached for her, and she slid across the seat and found comfort in his embrace. "I'll help you," he whispered.

She supposed that he didn't realize how much he already had. Farrah felt unworthy of this good man, but as she stayed tucked into his warm arms and breathed in the masculine scent of his skin, she prayed that she could somehow be the woman he deserved.

TUESDAY CAME, AND WITH IT FARRAH'S APPOINTMENT WITH Dr. Kenna. Farrah had spent several sessions with the redheaded therapist, and she really liked her. So she accepted the water bottle she'd been offered and looked at the pictures of Dr. Kenna's children while she waited.

For the first time since she'd started seeing someone, Farrah felt like she had a lot to say. The first couple of sessions had been strained while Dr. Kenna asked her questions Farrah didn't want to answer.

But she'd stayed. She hadn't stormed out or refused to come back, though she'd wanted to do both. Then she'd think of Darren and remind herself of why she needed to be here. If she really wanted him in her life, she needed to get it all cleaned up before he could move in.

"Farrah, come on back." The doctor smiled at her from the doorway, and Farrah grinned back. "You look good today." Dr. Kenna had been blessed with sharp, green eyes that didn't miss a single detail. Growing up with her as a mom would've probably been torture.

"I feel good today," Farrah said, taking a seat on the couch opposite the one Dr. Kenna sat on.

"Tell me why." She didn't take notes. She didn't hold anything. She sometimes had chocolate almonds she snacked on, or a bottle of pink lemonade, almost like she was simply spending time with a friend.

"I think I've finally told Darren everything." Bubbles of excitement formed in her chest, and she felt...giddy. She proceeded to tell Dr. Kenna about her conversations with Darren, her decision to buy horses and get riding with him, her time with some of the women in town at bunko night.

Her throat felt dry and her water had long been drunk

by the time she stopped talking. Dr. Kenna had listened, showing a smile when she needed to, or gesturing for Farrah to continue. She edged a bit farther forward on the seat now.

"Farrah, I'm a little bit worried about everything you told me."

Some of Farrah's giddiness fled. "What do you mean?"

"I fear...I'm just worried that you're taking on too much, too soon."

Farrah had not been expecting that. She leaned back into the couch, the wind that had been propelling her along suddenly gone.

"Remember how we were going to take things one at a time?" Dr. Kenna cleared her throat and stood. She retrieved a small notebook from her desk and handed it to Farrah. "Let me find you a pen."

A moment later, Farrah was armed and ready to write.

"Without thinking about it, without analyzing anything, I want you to write one-word answers to what I ask you. All right?"

Farrah trusted Dr. Kenna, so she nodded even as a blip of concern passed through her. What if she couldn't think of the right word? What if nothing came to mind?

"If you can't think of anything, just say pass, and we'll move on."

Farrah nodded, her throat too tight to speak anymore.

"One word." Dr. Kenna perched on the edge of the couch again, her pencil skirt pulling across her knees. "What are you hoping to gain from our therapy sessions?"

Farrah scribbled CLARITY across the top of the page and glanced back to the doctor.

"How can you get what you want?"

WORK got written next.

"What will it take to get what you want?"

Farrah almost wrote *work* again, but thankfully, her mind thought of TIME, and she put that instead. She wasn't sure if she could use the same word more than once or not, and she didn't want to ask.

"Who can help you get what you want?"

So many names came to Farrah's mind. Her mom. Her dad. Dr. Kenna. Darren.

She printed the last one, liking how his name looked on her paper of very important questions. Cocking her head, she admired the letters for an extra moment before turning her attention back to Dr. Kenna.

"What will you lose if you don't get what you want?"

Another hard question, with more than one answer.

"The first thing you think of," Dr. Kenna said.

Farrah wrote.

"All right. Let's see what you've got." She reached for the notebook and took it from Farrah, who was still unsure if she'd written the right answer on the last question.

"Good," the doctor murmured. "It will take work and time to get the clarity you're looking for Farrah." She glanced up and met Farrah's eye. "But this is what worries me. This right here." She turned the notebook and showed Farrah what she'd already seen.

Darren's name twice.

"How can he help you if you're scared to lose him?"

"I'm not scared—"

"You haven't even told me anything about you today. It was all about him."

She blinked and shook her head. "I mentioned the bunko. I'm making new friends in town."

Dr. Kenna put the notebook on the table beside her. "And you should. And I'm not saying Darren's bad for you. I'm saying that it's really hard to be what someone else wants you to be, when you don't know who you are yet."

Farrah wasn't exactly sure she understood what Dr. Kenna was saying, but she nodded like she did. "So I should…?"

"I can't tell you what you should do." She leaned back and crossed her legs, those eyes ever watchful. "But I know you've made great progress by focusing on *you* for the past several weeks. I'd hate to see that lost because you're focused on…something else, be that making friends or horseback riding with Darren."

Farrah felt like she'd been doused with a bucketful of ice water. Her mouth worked, but no sound came out.

"Think about what I said," Dr. Kenna said. "I could be wrong. Maybe you're doing just great, and all these big decisions you've made are fine." She smiled, a happy gesture that usually calmed Farrah's racing heart. Today though, it only added fuel to the firestorm inside her chest. "And we'll meet again next week."

Next week.

Farrah stood and shook the other woman's hand. She made it downstairs to her car. She drove home. Bolt greeted her inside with purrs and a rub along her calves. She normally bent down and stroked him, got his food and water bowls refreshed, and figured out what to eat for dinner.

Tonight, she made it to the couch and collapsed. The tabby leapt up beside her and curled into her lap. Farrah absently stroked his fur, wondering why writing Darren's name down twice was bad.

He *could* help her.

She *was* afraid of losing him.

Closing her eyes, she leaned her face toward the ceiling. She had never needed more clarity than she did right now, not even when she'd discovered she was pregnant with someone's baby she wasn't married to.

She'd come back from that.

She could figure this out too.

Dear Lord....

CHAPTER
SEVENTEEN

Darren loved the cooler weather of autumn. It was his favorite time of year, no matter where he and his brothers had worked. Reno didn't really have a fall season, and he'd missed it while there.

But Vermont did, and he loved the crisp morning air, the chill in the blue sky as the sun rose toward its pinnacle. The scent of leaves and dirt and pumpkin-flavored things. He enjoyed working outside when the weather was cooler, and he'd spent the last several evenings at the Bybee's, helping them chop wood for their boutique.

They needed it to keep the water temperature at a toasty eighty-two degrees all winter long. He'd eaten dinner with them every night, but Farrah had never stayed.

He hadn't seen much of her at all, though she texted him back when he contacted her. As he practically fell into his chair after the last load of wood had been stored, Corey said, "You work yourself too hard."

He gave her a lazy grin and reached for the rolls he'd smelled when he'd arrived earlier that afternoon. "I like to work hard."

"Don't give the boy trouble about working hard," Jim said.

"I'm not giving him trouble." Corey nudged the butter dish closer to Darren. "I'm just saying he has his own farm to look after."

"Not my farm," Darren corrected her. He'd toyed with the idea of buying one, but nothing had come together in his mind. He loved Steeple Ridge and the horses there, and for now, it was where he fit.

"Do you want a farm?" Jim asked.

"I don't know." Darren volleyed his gaze from Corey to Jim and back. "What's goin' on?" She was definitely wearing a look that said something, but Darren didn't know what.

"Nothing's going on." She lifted her chin. "Let's say grace so we can eat. Corn doesn't stay hot for long, you know."

Jim chuckled and said the prayer over the food. Darren barely heard him. He didn't like the unsettled feeling he had, and he hated it even more that he felt it here at the Bybees. This place had become a refuge for him, and he craved that peace, that solidity, that comfort.

So though Corey had made roast beef and crispy potatoes—two of his favorite foods—he could only scoop them onto his plate. He couldn't eat them. "Corey," he said. "*Something* is going on."

"Meagan doesn't want the farm," Jim said, tucking into his own food like he'd simply said the sky is blue. He chewed while Darren tried to work out what that meant. "Corey's fishing to see if you want it." He gave his wife a wry glare. "I told her she should just come right out and ask you, but well, we all have our own tactics."

Darren could only stare at Corey, who wore a tiny smile. She lifted one shoulder as if to say *Well?*

Through a narrow throat, Darren said, "Meagan loves this farm. She works here every day."

"She wants to raise her twins, not grow cilantro." Jim stated it matter-of-factly, but Corey flinched.

"She's having twins?"

"She just found out." The joy on Corey's face wasn't hard to find. "And she should stay home and take care of those babies. The doctor said they're going to be preemies." She pushed the cobs of corn closer to him. "Go on, Darren. Aren't you hungry?"

He looked at his food, then the corn. He scooped some onto his plate, because Corey expected him to. "So... Meagan's not coming back to the farm at all?"

Jim's face said no, and Corey vocalized it.

"But she's still here right now," Darren said. "Does she really run the whole thing?"

"No, she just does the botanical boutique," Corey said, spearing her husband with a look that said they'd had this conversation many times. "We need someone to run the farm."

"I'm—"

"Sixty-eight years old."

Darren took that opportunity to stuff his mouth full of roast beef. After all, he didn't get to get into this argument when it wasn't his.

But what about taking over a farm that wasn't his? Could he do that? Did he even want to?

And Darren knew that he did. That if Jim offered him the farm at a fair price, he'd buy it. Heck, he wanted it even if Jim asked too much for it.

The meal ended, and Jim started to clear the dishes. His nightly ritual. He'd start the coffee and clean up what Corey had made. Once, he'd told Darren that stacking the dishes in the sink was the least he could do for Corey, who kept the entire household running.

Darren leaned back in his chair, satisfied physically but his mind still churning. "How much are you asking for the farm?"

Jim paused near the doorway, his hands full. He smiled at Corey, who sat beaming at Darren.

"Oh, Darren, we'd love for you to have it."

"How much?"

"Jim hasn't specified a number." She stood too and came around the table to run her hand down the side of Darren's face. "He wants this farm to be yours so badly. He just won't say it out loud. So I said it for him."

Darren's emotions tangled up and balled in his throat. He nodded once, because he thought if he did more than that, the tears would overflow. His heart swelled with how much he loved Corey and Jim.

"Farrah won't stay for dinner," Corey said next, causing a different kind of pain to radiate through his body. "Do you know why?"

"I—" He cleared his throat. "I've spoken to her this week. She's a bit...distant, but nothing seems too off." He wasn't sure if texting counted as speaking, but Corey nodded, picked up a handful of dishes and followed Jim into the kitchen.

He pulled out his phone as Corey and Jim started singing together in the kitchen. Darren really wanted to have a life like theirs, one filled with dinner in the evenings, and songs in front of the sink, and love and laughter all year round.

Farrah answered, and she sounded tired. Maybe that was why she'd been leaving the farm before dinner. "Hey, sweetheart," he said, his voice almost a coo. "How are you? We've been missing you at dinner this week."

"Yeah, I've had tons of yard work to be ready for winter."

"You really want to retain that beautification award, don't you?"

"If I don't win twice in a row, people will think my green thumb is a fluke."

He chuckled. "So I already ate, but maybe you wouldn't mind the company?"

She took longer to answer than Darren liked, and that distance he'd commented on roared between them.

He turned away from the kitchen though he could still hear Jim and Corey singing. "I have something I want to talk to you about."

"Oh, yeah, I have something I want to talk to you about too."

Relief seeped through him. "Great, so I'll stop by for a few minutes."

When he got to Farrah's, the evidence of her work on the bushes, the shrubs, and the trees lay on the curb. He needed her prowess with a pair of tree shears out at Steeple Ridge.

Or maybe the Bybee's....

A smile slipped across his face as he mounted the steps. He knocked on the door, and Farrah took her sweet time answering the door. When she did, she wore one work glove crusted with dirt and carried the other. "Hey, I was in the backyard. Bolt kept scratching at the glass." She gave him a quick smile but stepped out of his reach so he couldn't kiss her hello.

Until that moment, he'd thought he might have been imagining the distance she'd put between them. She tucked her hair and ducked her head as he stepped inside.

"Everything okay?"

"Mm hm." But she wouldn't look at him, and alarms started sounding in his head.

"Yeah, I don't think so." He stopped two feet inside her house and shoved his hands in his pockets. Maybe if he'd spent more than five minutes with her this week, he'd have realized a chasm had opened between them. But he'd been busy too.

"Talk to me, Farrah," he said as she retreated into the kitchen and turned her back to him so she could wash her hands.

She'd told him once that he was impatient and pushy, and he refused to be either of those in this moment. So he waited, silent and still, by the door so he could make a quick escape if he needed to.

The fact that he thought he might need to escape raised another red flag in his mind.

She exhaled, turned, and leaned into the counter. "I think—I need...."

Darren breathed. Tried to calm his hammering heart. Waited for her to continue. At least if she broke up with him now, he'd be able to see her face as she did it. Last time, she'd sent a text that had to be broken up into five messages, berating him for his actions, his audacity, his attitude.

She wouldn't answer his calls, and he'd ended up apologizing to her voicemail a dozen times.

Farrah walked toward him, gathering up her hair and knotting it into a loose bun on top of her head. "I need to take things one at a time."

"Yeah, mm-hm. You said that."

Tears filled her beautiful eyes, and Darren hated that he couldn't soothe her. In a flash—a quick moment of thought—he wondered if she was simply too broken for a relationship. He couldn't believe he'd fallen in love with her all over again.

"Darren, I—" She threw her hands up. "It's not your turn."

His chest caved in on itself, and he felt like someone had dumped red ants in his boots. He needed to leave. Now.

"All right." He reached for the doorknob.

Farrah leapt in front of him and peered up at him with a tear-stained face. "All right?"

"What do you want from me, Farrah?" His fingers curled into fists. "I told you I love you. I told you we could unpack your baggage one item at a time. I—I—don't know what else you want from me." His voice cracked, and he drew in a breath that didn't calm him in the slightest.

"I don't know either."

He nodded and couldn't stop. "All right then. You call me when you know." This time, when he made to step past her, she let him go. Every step away from her felt like a knife in the heart.

"Darren," she called after him. "Don't go."

He turned back, apparently enjoying the extreme torture of getting his heart ripped out. She ran down the front steps and he swept her into his arms. She cried against his chest, and he held her right there on the sidewalk while she did.

"I'm sorry," she mumbled. "I'm a huge mess, and it's just not fair to you when I just can't—I can't—I don't want to hurt you." She pulled back. "That makes sense, doesn't it?"

Unable to speak, he shook his head. It made no sense. Breaking up with her hurt. Holding her when she wasn't his hurt. Not being able to discuss a possible purchase of the Bybee's farm hurt.

"I have to go," he said.

"You had something to tell me."

"I—" He released her and stepped back, his heart absolutely fissuring, a bunch of tiny little cracks spreading out and up and down, the way ice did just before it broke completely. "I can't."

He turned and practically ran to his truck, getting out of her driveway as quickly as possible. He just drove, trying to figure out what to do, where to go, how to be, without Farrah in his life.

She'd broken up with him before, but for some reason, he hadn't truly believed he'd never get her back. Now, though.... He really did wonder if she was even capable of being in a relationship like the one he wanted.

He drove through the dark streets, the shapes of old buildings, and mature trees, and the beautiful countryside slipping by without his full attention. Turn after turn, and Darren still couldn't sort out his thoughts.

His truck seemed to take him to Ben's house, where a light shone in the front window. Darren got out and walked slowly toward the steps. He sat on the concrete and looked up at the stars.

"Will I get her back?" he whispered to the cosmos, hoping God was there and would answer him. His brothers seemed to have found their happily-ever-afters without half this much pain. Of course, Darren didn't really know what Sam had gone through when he'd left Vermont—and the woman he'd loved—behind.

Nor did he know what it took to travel all the way across the country to California when your girlfriend had decided to stay here and keep her clinic.

And he had no idea how Ben had managed to slither in between Rae and her job.

So maybe his brothers hadn't had a yellow brick road to romance. Darren still felt like his journey was taking twice as long and the terrain was twice as rough.

That's because it's worth it, he thought. He wasn't sure if it was his own mind or a thought from a higher power, but it existed. He also wasn't sure if such a thing was really true. Farrah may never be ready to be with him, share her life with him, start a family with him.

"What are you doin' on my steps?" Ben nudged Darren with his boot and sat down beside him. "Rough night out at the Bybee's?"

"No." Darren shook his head. "Great night out there. Got all the wood in for the winter, and Jim practically offered me their farm."

Ben whistled through his teeth and let a few seconds pass in silence. "Wow. Like, they want you to buy it?"

"Yep."

"So…are you gonna buy it?"

"Yep." The word sprang from Darren's mouth without him having to overanalyze it. "I love that farm, and if I can have it…." A wave of gratitude overcame him. He couldn't actually believe he could have what the Bybee's did. But he wanted it. Wanted it real bad.

"So why are you sittin' on my steps?"

"Farrah broke up with me again."

"She did not." Ben's hushed tone conveyed more disbelief than Darren thought possible. "But I thought things were going well. She told Rae things were going well."

"She did?"

"At bunko night."

"That was over a week ago."

"So what? What happened?"

"Nothing." And Darren honestly couldn't think of a single thing. They'd spent time together. Talked. Texted. She'd come out to Steeple Ridge and told him about her father, about her inheritance. She was talking about buying horses, for crying out loud.

"Did she say why?"

"Said it wasn't my turn."

"What does that even mean?"

Darren didn't want to get into it. Number one, he respected Farrah's privacy, and it wasn't his place to tell Ben anything. "It means she came home with a lot of baggage, and she needs time to unpack it."

As he spoke, a calm, comforting feeling flowed over him with the gentleness of spring rain water. And he knew in that moment that he'd get Farrah back. She just needed time. Possibly a lot of it.

Help me be patient, he pleaded as Ben stood and said, "Well, you want coffee or anything? Rae brought home some of that dark roast from Montpelier."

"Yeah, I'll be in soon."

Ben left, and Darren contemplated the stars again. He found it amazing that someone had looked up and noticed patterns, found constellations, and named them. The sky just looked like a jumbled mess of lights to him. He desperately wanted God to show him the path to take—the one that would lead him back to Farrah for good.

But all he saw were stars.

"Thank you for the stars," he muttered as he stood. They were beautiful, and Darren did need to focus on being more thankful for what he did have, especially if he were to have the patience to endure what he didn't.

CHAPTER
EIGHTEEN

A week passed. Then two. Somehow a month went by, and Farrah only knew it because she opened her door one afternoon to find three children dressed in costumes. She had no idea it was Halloween, or where October had gone.

She went to work at the botanical boutique early in the morning, because she couldn't sleep. So she left earlier in the day. She told herself it wasn't because she didn't want to run into Darren, but she knew it was a lie.

And she hated that she was lying to herself. Knew that without being one-hundred percent truthful, she wouldn't be able to make the recovery necessary. Her mistakes in LA had taught her that much, at least.

She'd gotten the yard ready for winter, so when the first freezing rains and then snows descended on Island Park, she had nothing to do but watch the precipitation sluice down the windows.

Work on the farm happened. The sun rose. It set. Life seemed to go on around her, and Farrah didn't know how to grasp onto it, make it stop so she could get on.

She went to see her parents, and those visits provided bright pops of color in her otherwise drab existence. Thoughts of calling Darren circled incessantly, and she could never banish them completely.

Still, she didn't call him. He didn't call her either, and as winter really took its hold on the landscape, Farrah wondered if this was her new life.

But it's not really living, she thought. Dr. Kenna had asked her to focus on herself. Really get things worked out, fixed, and aligned in herself before adding Darren to the mix. But Farrah hadn't seen the therapist once since she'd broken up with Darren.

She arrived at the boutique on Friday morning, her breath steaming in front of her as she made her way from the parking lot to the door. Inside, it would be warm and humid, and she increased her pace as a stiff wind kicked up.

Behind her, the growl of a big truck sounded. Curious, she turned to see what was going on. A moving truck inched down the road, passing behind some trees that had lost their leaves at some point. Farrah hadn't even seen when. True remorse pulled through her, because she loved autumn in Vermont, and she'd completely missed it.

The truck stopped in front of the Bybee's house, and men started spilling from the cab. In the next moment, the back got opened, and Jim appeared. He shook hands with one of the men, and even from three hundred yards away, Farrah understood what was happening.

The Bybee's were moving.

Confusion cascaded through her with the force of a waterfall. Had they sold the farm? If so, to whom? And what would become of her?

So though her limbs felt encased in ice, she turned back the way she'd come and started walking toward the house. She bypassed the little lot where she parked every morning, and continued along the fence line to the dirt road that led to town.

"Corey?" she asked when she was still several paces away. "What's going on?"

Corey kept her hands in her pockets as she pulled her coat tighter against her body. A hint of unshed tears sat in her eyes. "Moving day." She couldn't seem to look away from the men as they hauled out boxes and stacked them on the porch.

"Where are you going?"

Corey focused on her now. "Farrah, we're moving into town." She spoke so slow, which only caused Farrah's bewilderment to double.

"Town?"

"We've spoken about this numerous times, dear." Corey withdrew her hand and put it on Farrah's arm. "Do you not remember?"

She shook her head, her nose so numb and her face practically frozen. "Where are you living?"

"We bought a nice condo in that newer building just south of downtown." She gazed at Farrah with pity and a healthy amount of concern in her eyes. "Farrah, you said Meredith lives in that building. Remember?" Her fingers tightened, and Farrah looked at where she was gripping her arm.

Problem was, she didn't remember.

"Do I have a job?" She blinked through the bitter cold, wondering what January would be like if mid-November was already this wicked cold.

Corey sighed, the sound somewhere between defeat and frustration. "Yes, dear. Meagan is going to stay home with her twins. We hired you full-time a month ago."

"What about…?" Farrah stalled as Darren came through the front door carrying a sizable credenza all by himself. He made it look easy, just like everything he did. But he wore some definite emotion on his face, and Farrah couldn't decipher it all before her view of him got blocked.

"Corey, I need you in here," Jim called from the porch, waving at her to join him in the house.

"Darren agreed to keep all the staff," Corey said. "It was part of the contract." She gave Farrah another sad smile, and went up the steps to see what her husband needed.

Darren.

Darren?

She inhaled sharply, like she'd been underwater for a long time and had just now broken the surface.

Darren bought the farm.

Darren will keep all the staff.

Darren will move in before Thanksgiving.

Darren, Darren, Darren.

Everything Corey and Jim had told her came rushing back, flooding her mind with words and filling her body with emotion.

Darren headed back up the steps too, only paces from her. He hadn't looked at her once. Hadn't spoken to her.

She felt so warm that she was sure her body heat would be steaming off of her. How much time had she lost? And what had she done in that time to move Darren up the list?

With a groan and a spike of anger, she realized she hadn't done anything. Hadn't worked on anything. That she was actually no closer to a solution for herself than she'd been when she'd broken up with him.

Whipping out her phone, she made a decision—maybe the first real decision in months. She called Dr. Kenna's office, and said, "I need the first available appointment."

Later that afternoon, she sat across from the therapist. She'd declined a drink and instead launched right into what she needed.

"You said I needed to figure out who I was."

"No, I said you didn't know who you were."

Same thing, in Farrah's opinion. She leaned forward. "How do I figure that out?"

"What have you tried?"

"Nothing." She'd done nothing since leaving this office weeks ago. Fury at herself roared through her with the strength of gravity. Why had she let someone else dictate to her what she should do?

"You've surely done something."

"I've seen my parents a couple of times."

"And how is that going?"

"Just fine." Farrah knew her parents loved her, and they weren't a problem anymore. She'd unpacked them, and while she should probably call them more often, she'd barely been functioning for the past month.

"Farrah." Dr. Kenna sighed, and for the first time since Farrah had started meeting with her, she sounded frustrated. "I want to ask you a question. I want you to spend the next week discovering the answer. And then we'll meet again."

She'd only been in the office for five minutes, but she nodded.

"Do you like you?"

"I—" Farrah stalled completely. She'd spent so much time worrying about what everyone else thought of her, that she hadn't stopped to ask herself why. Did it matter if she had a starring role?

It did to her father.

Did it matter that she was married when she was pregnant?

It did to her parents in Burlington.

Did she need the nicest clothes, the curled hair, all the makeup?

Yes, she thought. Because it hid who she really was. And if people saw who she really was, they wouldn't like her.

"Just think about it," Dr. Kenna said. "You need to like you. After that, it doesn't really matter what anyone else thinks."

"Even you?" Farrah managed to ask.

The doctor nodded, a soft smile on her lips. "Even me."

Farrah got up and left the office without another word. She got behind the wheel of her car and she drove. She loved the simple roads without any lines down the middle. She liked the old barns, the steeple on the brown-brick church. She liked the way the town felt old, established, cultured.

How she'd ever thought she could survive outside of Vermont was a mystery to her. She drove out to Steeple Ridge, but she didn't turn off to go to Darren's. He didn't live there anymore anyway. She didn't pull into the parking lot around the other side of the farm either. A single horse remained in the fenced pasture, and she slowed as she watched the magnificent brown and white creature graze.

She liked horses. They'd always spoken to her soul somehow. Maybe if she'd have stayed at the farm when she'd found out about her adoption, they would've been able to mend the broken pieces of her life.

Braking, she pulled to the side of the road. She wasn't sure if she liked herself, but she suddenly knew what she could do to find out.

THE FOLLOWING DAY, SHE DROVE THROUGH THE COUNTRYSIDE again, finding a few trees that had hung onto their leaves. Not many, but a few. She wondered why some held onto their leaves so tightly and some let go.

She desperately wanted to let go of some things. "Is it as easy as simply opening my fist and letting go?"

No one answered, and Dr. Kenna's question plagued her again.

Do you like you?

Farrah had looked in the mirror that morning for a long time. She saw her skin, her eyes, her hair, her nose, her lips. All the pieces of herself that made up her physical body. Apart from the miscarriage, she'd never been seriously ill or injured.

Gratitude had touched her heart, and she'd turned away from her reflection, the answer to her question a definite no.

She did not like her.

And if she had to list all the reasons why, they were all about the decisions she'd made, the things she'd done, and the people she'd hurt in her life. She'd tried to shower away some of the miserable feelings, but they remained.

So she'd called Meagan and said she was sick, and then she called her parents and asked if she could come stay with them for the weekend. They'd been thrilled, and Farrah half-expected a welcome-home parade when she arrived.

But her parents' house sat in silence, the sky gray all around it. Farrah stayed in the car and looked at the cream-colored brick. In the summer, her father worked hard to keep the rust stains from creeping up the side of the house, and her mother tended a garden equal in size to the house.

Her stomach grumbled, prompting Farrah to get out of

the car and go inside. The air held a note of winter and the hint of cinnamon as she walked toward the front door. A curtain fluttered, and her mother opened the door a few moments later.

"Farrah." She wore a warm smile and swept down the stairs to embrace Farrah.

Guilt pricked Farrah's heart, and tears gathered behind her eyes. She clung to her mother, and whispered, "I'm sorry, Mom."

Her mom didn't have to ask for what. No additional explanation needed. She patted Farrah's back, and her voice sounded higher when she said, "I made maple oatmeal cookies. Come on." She sniffed and wiped her eyes as she turned, but Farrah saw the storm of emotions on her face.

"Mom?" Farrah paused on the top step before entering the house. "Do you like me?"

Surprise stole across her mother's face, through her dark eyes that matched Farrah's so well. "Of course I do. I *love* you." She gestured for Farrah to come in out of the cold.

She did, pulling the door closed behind her. "But do you like me?" she pressed. "Even though I—"

"Farrah, I prayed for a daughter like you for a decade," her mother said, tears welling up and overflowing. She didn't even try to brush them away this time. "I loved you the moment I laid eyes on you, and yes, I've always liked you." She put a weathered, wrinkled hand on Farrah's arm and led her into the kitchen.

"You're a fun person. Remember when you were

learning all the bones in your health class, and you'd come home and say things like, 'My mandible is moving as I chew.'" She laughed, the sound throaty and conjuring up memories that had happened right here in this house.

Her parents were all Farrah had ever had. She'd abandoned them twelve years ago for reasons she didn't understand—until now.

"I felt like I'd lost you," she whispered into the last echoes of her mother's laughter.

"What was that?"

"I left Vermont, because I felt like I'd lost you. When I found out I wasn't really yours."

"Farrah." Her mom smiled warmly up at her. "You've always been ours. You'll always be ours."

"Hey, baby doll."

She turned into the comforting embrace of her father. He smelled like freshly buttered popcorn from the theater he owned, and she drew in a deep breath of him. "Hey, Dad."

"Your mom's right, you know." He stepped back and snagged a cookie from the cooling rack. "You may have left for a while, but we always knew you'd come home."

Farrah marveled at the pair of them. "I have all the letters and cards you sent," she whispered.

"We know." Her father exchanged a glance with her mom. "We don't need more apologies, Farrah." He sounded so sincere, so kind, when he said it. "As your mom said, you're the best thing that's ever happened to us."

"I haven't lost you." Farrah wasn't asking, but she needed to say it out loud to herself so she'd believe it.

That night, after her parents had gone to bed, Farrah swept all the makeup from her face. She pulled her hair back into a ponytail and looked into her brown eyes. "They like you," she whispered. They liked her without lip gloss. Without a job. Without any strings attached.

They'd forgiven her for abandoning them. For not responding to twelve years' worth of cards and letters. For trying to replace them with a man who had never wanted her.

"Why do I want *him* to like me?"

Gary Lewis had never liked Farrah. He hadn't even liked the idea of her. The only reason she'd been born was because her mother refused to end a life. She'd given hers for Farrah's, and Gary had given Farrah away.

"He didn't even know me," she said, watching her lips move in the mirror. "He didn't give me up because he didn't like me."

And why did it matter if that was the reason? He'd given her a wonderful gift. Two of them, actually. A mother and a father who loved her.

And who liked her.

She turned away from herself and went down the dark hall to her childhood bedroom. Her mother had gotten rid of the frilly purple curtains, and the butterfly bedspread. The pictures of Farrah and her horse remained, as did her trophies, medals, and sashes. Farrah let her fingers trail over the emblems of her past.

Her horses had always liked her, wild hair and too tight knees against their sides and everything.

She climbed into bed, her mind churning out one question.

But do you like you?

CHAPTER
NINETEEN

Darren had barely settled into his new home—most of which sat empty as he owned two pieces of furniture. A bed and a recliner—before he boarded a plane with Ben and flew to Billings.

Sam and Bonnie were hosting Thanksgiving dinner at their farm in Coral Canyon, and Logan and Layla were coming.

Rae was too far along in her pregnancy to fly, and she and her mother had volunteered to help out with the church meal. Pastor Gray sponsored a holiday meal for anyone who didn't have family in the area to celebrate with. "No one should have to eat alone on Thanksgiving," he'd said from the pulpit a few weeks ago. He was a master at getting people to volunteer to help others, and Darren half wished he could stay home and fry a turkey for the church get-together.

After all, he didn't really want to hash out why Farrah had broken up with him again. He'd texted the news to Logan, who had called. Darren had avoided the call, and Logan hadn't tried again.

He did send motivational texts all the time, almost to the point that when Darren's phone made its snappy ringtone he'd specifically chosen for Logan, dread filled his stomach.

He didn't need to see things like *She'll come around.*

Or *Be patient with her. Remember what happened when I wasn't patient with Layla?*

Or *Layla says she can talk to her. See how she's doing.*

Darren had finally responded to that one. *Don't let Layla talk to her. I'm fine. We're fine.*

He was anything but fine, living on his dream farm with the woman he loved as an employee. An employee who hadn't spoken to him in almost two months, but still. His desire to have Farrah on the farm with him sometimes threatened to drive him mad.

He'd heat something for dinner, only to think of her eating with him someday, and then his appetite would flee.

But as Ben navigated toward Coral Canyon on the east side of Yellowstone National Park, Darren knew he'd have to explain more of the situation to his brothers if he wanted them to stop asking questions.

The questions themselves didn't bother him. It was reliving the pain that still echoed in his heart. Remembering the agony in her eyes as she said it wasn't his turn. Experiencing the pure powerlessness he had over the situation.

Most days, he could just go to work around the farm and not have to think about Farrah. But as winter arrived, and there was less physical labor required, his distraction wouldn't last for much longer.

"Here we are." Ben pulled into the driveway at the blue farmhouse where they'd grown up. "I wish Rae had been able to come."

"I know, bro." Darren flashed Ben a sympathetic look and got out of the car. He collected his luggage and headed up the steps on the side of the house. The door opened to warmth, cheery yellow light, and the scent of milk and powder—like his new niece.

"We're here," he called, and the piano playing in the other room silenced. Sam made an appearance a moment later, followed by Bonnie, who carried a little bundle Darren really wanted to meet.

"Hey." Sam grinned as if Darren and Ben were celebrities. He crossed the distance to them and drew them into a double hug. "You made it. How was the flight?"

"Long," Ben complained at the same time Darren said, "Just fine."

"Logan just called. He said there's a storm coming in fast. They're hoping to beat it here."

Darren hoped they would too. He and Logan had been close growing up, and until Logan had moved to California last January, they'd never slept in two different rooms. He hadn't realized how powerful their twin bond was until his brother wasn't there.

Feeling overly emotional and nostalgic, he slowly approached Bonnie. She smiled down at the baby with such love—love that Darren felt burning through him too.

"This is Jacqueline," she said, tilting the little girl toward Darren. She had feathery dark hair, the exact same color as Sam's. "We're calling her Jackie."

Darren tore his eyes from the baby to his brother. "After Mom?"

Sam gazed at his daughter with unadulterated love and nodded, his throat working against his emotion.

Darren tried to swallow and couldn't. "Can I hold her?" His voice sounded choked, and he wasn't quite sure how to hold an infant, but Bonnie turned the baby into his arms effortlessly.

She gurgled and grunted, and Darren chuckled, wishing with everything inside him that he lived close enough to Sam and Bonnie to see Jackie every single day. Watch her grow up on this farm the way he had.

And he suddenly understood why Sam had felt such a powerful call to return to Coral Canyon and their father's farm.

"She's beautiful," he murmured, automatically bouncing the baby like his fatherly instincts were alive and well.

"We sure like her," Sam said, clapping his hand on Ben's back as he joined them.

Darren passed Jackie to Ben, who cooed at her like his baby had already been born. "What should we name our little girl?" he asked.

"You're havin' a girl?" Sam asked.

Ben grinned and nodded. "We've known for a while, but wanted it to be a surprise. Don't tell Rae I told you." He swayed with baby Jackie, the little two-month-old seeming to smile in her sleep.

Darren turned back toward the door and the steps that led down to the basement. "So I'll be in my old room?"

"It flooded last spring," Sam said. "It's brand new down there. Let me show you." He led the way as the brothers went downstairs, and Darren's breath caught in his throat. This basement wasn't anything like what they'd had as boys. Light gray paint on the walls and bright white trim kept the airy atmosphere of upstairs present even underground.

"The windows are huge," he said as Ben came thundering down the steps, obviously having passed Jackie back to Bonnie upstairs.

"I had them enlarged," Sam said. "It's so much brighter, don't you think?"

"Yeah." Ben spoke with the same reverent tone that Darren felt in his soul. His mother would've loved a basement like this. She was always telling their dad that it was too dark down there, and she worried about her sons sleeping in a damp, dark dungeon.

New carpet stretched from wall to wall, and Darren found a queen-size bed in each of the two bedrooms downstairs. Fresh linens adorned the beds, and there were even live plants.

"Bonnie has a green thumb." Sam gazed at the plants like they were his children. "I don't know how she keeps them alive down here, but she does it." Love colored his voice, and Darren's throat tightened. He cleared it, and set his bag on the end of the bed in his and Logan's old bedroom.

"I put Logan and Layla upstairs with me and Bonnie," Sam said. "You and Ben can have the basement. Then you won't hear Jackie scream in the middle of the night."

Ben nodded like it was no big deal, but Darren wanted to sequester himself in the bedroom and wait out the weekend. He didn't want to be relegated to the basement because he was single. It wasn't a bachelor pad, for heaven's sake.

Ben left, leaving his bag in the remodeled living room, leaving Darren alone with Sam. "You okay?" Sam asked, his voice low and filled with concern.

Darren collapsed onto the end of the bed next to his suitcase. "Some days, I don't know." He ran both hands over his face, pushing off his cowboy hat and pulling his fingers through his hair. "Some days, yeah, I'm okay."

"What's today?" Sam asked, leaning into the doorway as if they were talking about the weather.

"Today's unknown."

"I've had those days."

Darren was sure he had. It didn't make his heart hurt less or his muscles release. But at least someone else knew what it felt like to be alone. While Rae wasn't here physically, she was still with Ben.

Out of the Buttars brothers, only Darren was still alone. And he'd never felt it more powerfully than he did sitting in a room he didn't recognize.

"Stay down here as long as you want," Sam said. "You'll know when Logan gets here."

Darren appreciated Sam's brotherhood. The way he'd always taken care of the family. The way he seemed to know when to push and when to back off. Still, something seethed inside him, and he fell back onto the bed, wondering if he could simply sleep away the next four days and then fly back to the cozy, quaint, quiet farm that he'd just bought.

Sometime later, the crunch of tires on gravel forced Darren into a sitting position. Logan had arrived, and with him, Darren knew his reprieve from answering questions had ended.

He sighed as he stood, straightened his hat, and started for the stairs. He almost wanted to get everything out in the open so his family could help him come to terms with things. He reached the top of the stairs at the same time Logan tried to knock him down them again.

"Darren." Logan's eyes sparkled, and the hole in Darren's life that his brother had always been able to fill disappeared.

"Hey, bro." Darren grabbed onto Logan and hugged him. "You look tanner than I remember." They clapped each other loudly on the back.

"The California sun is amazing." Logan laughed. "You really should come out at Christmas. It doesn't snow or anything."

Darren loved Vermont in the winter, but he just smiled and said, "I really should come at Christmas."

After all, anything would be better than hanging his

single stocking by the fireplace and buying himself a gift to put under the tree. When he'd bought the Bybee's farm, he'd imagined it filled with family, with friends, with faith.

And with Farrah.

But the only thing there was him.

"So, let's talk about Farrah." Logan cast a glance over his shoulder. "Layla's been dyin' to solve your problems. I think she wants you to be happy more than I do."

Darren smiled. Layla had a good air about her, and she'd always helped people in Island Park. How his brother had managed to marry her boggled Darren's mind.

"I'm happy," Darren said, which only elicited a laugh from Logan.

"Oh, bro. I can take one look at you and know you're not happy. I've been there, remember?" He started through the kitchen, where Ben was elbow-deep in pretzel dough. The smell of yeast and salt mixed with the pine tree-scented candle burning atop the piano. Darren wrinkled his nose at the odd combination.

"Here he is, Lay." Logan announced Darren's presence as if Layla had been looking all over for him for hours.

She sprang from the couch—surprisingly agile with the baby in her arms—and engulfed Darren in a hug. He held her for a moment, chuckling at her exuberance.

"How are you?" She held onto his biceps as she stepped back, examining his face. "Oh, he's bad."

"I'm fine," Darren said, casting a glance at Bonnie. She too wore pity in her eyes, and Darren didn't need that. "Honestly, you guys. I'm okay."

"So what happened?" Layla asked, and that was the question that launched the next two hours of conversation. By the end of it, Darren was no closer to a solution, but he also didn't feel like someone had clawed their way into his chest and ripped out his heart.

So, progress.

He went to bed before everyone else after volunteering to help Sam with the early morning chores the next day. In the new and unused bedroom, Darren fell to his knees and prayed. Prayed to express his gratitude for his family. For his safety. For his health.

At the very end, after thanking God for all he'd been given, Darren finally allowed himself to utter, "Please help Farrah."

It was all he'd been asking for since they'd broken up. He didn't know exactly what she needed, but the Lord did. He didn't know how far she'd come, or how far she still had to go. But the Lord did.

And Darren could do this one thing for her. He hadn't missed a night of pleading for her in almost two months. Satisfied with his offering, he climbed into bed and turned out the light. Farrah lingered in his mind, swirling around as he moved from conscious to unconscious, and he fell asleep with a smile slipping across his lips.

DARREN CAME IN FROM THE EARLY MORNING CHORES ON Thanksgiving Day, his face frozen from the cold. The strong scent of pumpkin pie spice hit him in the gut and he glanced to where Bonnie and Layla stood at the stove, at least five pots and pans covering the burners.

"Oh, there he is." Bonnie turned and wiped her hands on her apron. "Sam said you would make the table decorations." She picked up a package of striped shortbread cookies and looked at him expectantly.

Darren had once put together a pilgrim hat from the cookies, miniature peanut butter cups, and frosting. He'd been ten, and his mother had asked him to do it every year until the year she died. That year, Sam had done it, but Darren had picked up the habit again the next year.

His throat tightened at Sam's thoughtfulness. "Yeah, sure. Of course."

Bonnie beamed at him and bent to pick up Jackie's pacifier. She stopped the swing where the baby rocked and stuck it back in the fussy infant's mouth. "And Sam said you have to pick the Christmas tree for the farmhouse."

Darren froze. "No, I don't want to do that."

Her face fell as she finished tending to Jackie and faced him again. "Why not?"

"Because I don't live here." He looked over her shoulder to where Layla stood, stirring but obviously listening. "I'm going to California for Christmas. I won't even see it."

"He said your mom put up a huge Christmas tree the day after Thanksgiving every year." Bonnie's hands flitted around her hair.

"She did," Darren said. "So?"

"So he wants to do that," Bonnie said. "While all of you brothers are here. Sort of continue the tradition."

Layla turned down the heat on one of the burners and said, "We'll have a teeny, tiny tree to go with our teeny, tiny apartment." She threw a smile over her shoulder. "So you better get your Christmas tree spirit here."

Darren didn't need to get his Christmas tree spirit in Wyoming. He had a whole farm full of trees in Vermont. Some pine, just like what they'd find in the forests nearby the farmhouse. But he didn't want to argue. Sam wanted to continue their parents' traditions, and Darren wouldn't stand in the way of that, even if he wasn't feeling up to it.

He nodded and gestured downstairs. "I'm going to go shower." He escaped downstairs before the women could ask him to stay by making up a chore they needed his help with. Sam hadn't come in from the stable yet, and Darren hadn't seen Logan at all that morning. He liked to sleep late, and he'd take the afternoon shift with the animals.

By the time Darren went back upstairs to make the pilgrim hats, the living room and kitchen were full of people. Sam sat at the piano and played softly while the women cooked and Ben baked pretzels and Jackie rocked in her swing.

Logan was setting the table, and he gestured Darren over. "So who has Rambo this weekend?"

"He's with Tucker and Missy." Darren opened the package of cookies. "He's doin' great, Logan. I think he might like me more than you by the time you get back."

Logan chuckled and folded another napkin. Darren stared at the embroidered B on the light blue cloth. A vivid memory spilled forward, rendering him silent for a few moments. He and Logan had been playing outside one spring day after school. They were probably in fourth or fifth grade, and they weren't supposed to play in the equipment barn with the tractors.

But they were, and Logan had sliced open his forearm on a spoke. Darren had run to the house for help and he'd burst in on his mom while she sat in the armchair, her needle flying in and out of that blue cloth, putting in that white, flowery B.

B for Buttars.

She'd brought the napkin with her as she followed him out to the barn. She'd pressed that blue cloth right on Logan's wound, and then she'd taken him into the house before loading him and Darren into the car and going to the hospital.

She'd left Sam in charge of Ben, and Darren had never seen the napkin again.

"Is that a full set?" he asked Logan, his mouth barely moving.

"What?" Logan reached into a basket and pulled out another napkin.

"Those napkins. How many are there?"

"Twelve."

Darren nodded. So she'd finished the set and never used them. He wondered why. He wondered what they could've been for.

"There are green ones too," Logan said. "And a set of yellow. And tan. I think mine were the yellow ones." He folded the corner in, and Darren wondered how he'd learned to do that. "These are Sam's."

"We all have a set?"

Logan nodded, obviously not nearly as emotionally invested in this conversation as Darren was. "Yeah. Mom wanted us to be Buttars." He glanced up. "Don't you remember her saying that all the time? 'Be Buttars, you guys. It means something to be a Buttars.'" He chuckled and shook his head.

Darren vaguely remembered that. He couldn't fathom why he could remember her stitching the napkins and not that she'd made each of her sons a set. Couldn't immediately recall that she'd always told them it meant something to be a Buttars.

"I think she was right," Darren said as he smeared the first bit of frosting on the cookie. "It does mean something to be a Buttars."

Logan nodded, folded the last napkin and set it in place. "Yeah, I think it does too." He left Darren to finish the table decorations, and then they all sat down to eat.

"All right, all right." Sam stood at the head of the table the way their father had for each meal. He always shared something that had happened on the farm that day, and Sam looked like he might cry.

"It's so good to have everyone here." He glanced at Ben. "I mean, not everyone." His eyes landed on Darren too. "But hopefully, one day, everyone can be here." He cleared his throat. "But all the brothers are here, and I think we should go around the table and share one thing we're grateful for this year."

He sat and tucked himself under the table. "I'll go first. I'm grateful for family."

"That's too easy." Logan scoffed. "I'm grateful for a brother who takes good care of my dog." He reached for Layla's hand. "And a wife that lets me follow my dreams."

Bonnie said she was grateful for new beginnings, her eyes fastened to her baby, and Layla said she was grateful for the opportunity to experience different things. Ben copied Sam, and said he was grateful for family and the chance to be a dad, and then only Darren hadn't gone.

Everyone looked at him expectantly, and he picked up the pilgrim hat that still looked like a child had made it. "I'm grateful for traditions."

And he was. He felt steeped in them here at the farmhouse where he'd grown up, and it was one of the things he loved most about the Bybee's farm. Jim and Corey had traditions, even if it was simply eating dinner at six o'clock every evening. And Jim clearing the table. And the two of them singing while they did the dishes.

Darren loved that farm and everything on it because of the rich tradition it held. He wanted to add to it, grow it, cultivate it into his own legacy.

It means something to be a Buttars.

He hadn't felt whole in a while, like Farrah's departure from his life had left holes in his soul. But sitting around the table with his family, some of that ache disappeared. Still, whenever he thought about who would be by his side as he expanded and enriched the existing traditions at the Bybee farm, it was always Farrah.

Farrah, who had fallen in love with the farm and the boutique almost as fast as Darren had.

So as turkey and mashed potatoes got passed around the table, Darren sent a quick prayer heavenward that Farrah was somewhere safe and inviting this Thanksgiving, and that she'd feel a measure of happiness the same way Darren did.

CHAPTER
TWENTY

After too much turkey and two pieces of pumpkin pie, Farrah opened her laptop to fight off the effects of tryptophan. Or maybe she'd simply eaten so much she felt like she needed to sleep for days.

No matter what, she wanted to show her parents the agribusiness degree she'd researched at the University of Vermont. "It's right here in Burlington," she said, turning the computer toward them. Her mom sipped her coffee and peered at the screen.

"It goes right along with what I already do at the Bybee's." She didn't bother to call the farm Darren's, though she should. He hadn't renamed it yet. Hadn't put up a new sign. She'd watched him toss two bags into the back of his truck a couple of days ago and rumble down the lane toward the highway. He'd probably gone to either Sam's or Logan's for the holiday. The farm had seemed empty without him there, though there were farmhands coming to take care of the horses as usual.

Farrah had come to Burlington on Tuesday night, and she was staying until Sunday. "I've already applied to the program," she said. "And I think I'm going to move up here."

Her dad's eyebrows shot up and he switched his gaze from the screen to her face. "Really? You'd leave that yard you've cultivated?" He cocked his head to the side at her casual shrug. "Farrah, you love that yard."

And she did. She couldn't deny that. "It's a thirty-seven minute drive from my house to the university. If I live on the south side of town, I can get to work in fifteen minutes." Having the farm halfway between the two cities was a real plus, and Farrah hadn't been as excited about anything as she was about starting college. At least not for a long time.

"The south side?" Her mom made a face. "Farrah, that's not the best neighborhood."

"There's lot of new development," Farrah said. She'd already looked at condos and townhomes going in near the historical museums and other old buildings that used to be the heart of Burlington. "I think the neighborhood is changing."

So maybe she'd driven by it on her way into town. She almost felt giddy from the excitement of doing something with her life that felt right.

"How are you going to afford something new?" her mom asked. "And pay for college?"

Farrah sucked in a breath, the lie easily forming in her

mind. She shoved it out, pushed hard against the desire to keep the secret she'd had for eighteen months. But she'd already told Darren, and that alone gave her strength.

"I, uh, actually, I have quite a bit of money from my time in LA."

"You do?" her parents asked at the same time. They exchanged a glance and it was her dad who added, "I didn't think you'd been cast in anything major."

"I never was." In fact, she'd hardly worked there, unless waitressing at a breakfast bar counted. "This money is from my...from Gary Lewis." He wasn't her dad. Her real dad was sitting in front of her, his mouth hanging partially open.

"What?" her mom asked.

"Gary Lewis was my biological father. He passed away last year, and he didn't have a will or any family. I had my original birth certificate, and I'd made contact with him several times, and well, the lawyer said I got his estate."

Her mom pushed away from the table and took a couple of steps back. Her hand fluttered near her throat. "Oh, I—"

"It's okay, Mom." Farrah stood and put both her hands on her mom's shoulders. "Its just money. He wasn't my dad."

The resulting silence felt powerful and yet peaceful. Her dad joined them, and Farrah hugged her parents. "You guys are my mom and dad." She smiled, finally feeling like she belonged to them and they belonged to her. "And I really think there's a condo near the lake that has my name on it."

Farrah rode the elevator up to Meredith's condo, a stable of nerves in her stomach. She hadn't attended bunko night since September. She may have been invited; she couldn't really remember.

But she'd been feeling more and more like herself with every passing day. She'd been accepted into the agribusiness program at the University of Vermont, and she'd put down money on a condo on the top floor of a south-facing building. It had a lake-view.

Not only that, but Meagan was going to take a break from all the bunko next year to focus on being a mom to twins, and she'd offered her spot in the group to Farrah.

She'd accepted it, and the group was meeting tonight for a fun-filled dinner party with dice, and laughter, and planning for next year.

She'd seen Darren around the farm, carefully tending to the new maple trees he'd planted. Because of her slump, she didn't know exactly when he'd planted them, but by covertly bringing up the subject with Meagan, she'd learned that he'd put in the grove of thirty trees in mid-October. Jim Bybee had helped, and she'd seen him coming round the farm from time to time.

When he came, he and Darren disappeared into the trees or they sat on the front porch and whittled. Farrah pretended not to know that Darren was only a few hundred yards from where she worked each day.

He never came into the boutique while she was there, but she knew he'd been there. There was evidence of more firewood stacked neatly in the bin whenever it started to get low. A trellis broke one afternoon, and she'd spent hours transferring strawberry plants to another rack. The following morning, the trellis had been fixed. She never mentioned anything to anyone about the needed repairs. He simply paid attention and took care of things.

He'd always been that way. Attentive. Action-oriented.

She adored that about him, and she hoped he was getting enough sleep. With how much work it took to run a farm, he probably wasn't. And that set her to worrying, which always made her realize how ridiculous she was being.

She was worried about a man she couldn't talk to.

The elevator doors slid open, and a door stood ajar halfway down the hall. It was definitely Meredith's apartment, because holiday music poured into the building and the scent of sugar and almond punch wafted into the air.

Meredith came through the door and saw Farrah. A smile formed on her face. "Hey, Farrah. Haven't seen you in a couple of months."

Farrah managed to return the grin. "Yeah, but I guess Rae isn't feeling well tonight?"

Meredith shrugged though a vein of worry skated through her eyes. "I guess not. She said she wants November next year. Her baby will be almost a year old by then, and she's been baking up a storm, I guess." She reached for Farrah and slung her arm around her shoulders. "Come on in. What month are you thinking of hosting?"

"Oh, I don't know," Farrah said. Most women had busy

times at work, or a husband with a schedule, or kids to deal with. She just had the boutique and her upcoming classes.

But that's okay, she told herself. She wasn't any less important because she didn't have a busy job, a husband, or a family.

"May is fun," Meredith said. "I did a Cinco de Mayo night a couple of years ago."

"That does sound fun." They moved into the apartment, where only a few of the girls waited. Farrah shrugged out of her coat and filled a plastic cup with Rae's famous punch. She'd taken one delicious gulp when she remembered Rae wasn't actually here.

"Hey, who made the punch?" she asked.

Meredith's whole face lit up. "I got the recipe."

Aria and Hazel gasped. Cheryl said, "You did not."

"She swore her mother would never give it out." Michelle looked into her cup like perhaps the punch was fake.

"She felt so bad about not being able to come that she told me." Meredith grinned like she'd discovered gold. "And it's so easy, you guys."

"So are you going to tell us?"

"What? And have this punch at every picnic in town? No. No way." Meredith shook her head. "First off, Rae would kill me, and second, this is a bunko night tradition. We can't have the whole town drinking it."

Farrah laughed with a couple of the other women. She drank her punch and put her name on the schedule to host in June next year. "Oh, I'm moving to Burlington," she said. "Is that a problem? I can find somewhere to host here if it is."

"Burlington?" Cheryl's perfectly sculpted eyebrows rose. "What are you doing in Burlington?"

"I'm going back to school." A sense of pride inflated Farrah's chest.

"Are you selling your house here?" Meredith asked.

"In the spring," she said.

"I want to buy it," she said quickly, glancing at the other girls. "Me and Denny have been talking about getting something without shared walls."

"Really?" Farrah asked. "Well, I could sell it now, I guess. I just thought spring would be a better time."

"What does Darren think of you moving to Burlington?" Aria batted her eyelashes and sipped her punch like she hadn't just asked a loaded question.

"I'm not—we're not dating anymore."

"The whole town knows that," Aria said, setting her cup on the counter. "But what does he think of it?"

"I don't know." Farrah glanced around, noting the sympathy in her friend's eyes. "I don't actually talk to him."

"He owns the farm where you work," Michelle said. "How do you avoid him?"

It was actually Darren who moved like a ninja around the farm. Farrah tried to find a reason not to tell these women anything. But she wanted them in her life, the same way she'd wanted to share all her secrets with Darren.

"I don't know," she said again. "He doesn't come into the boutique while I'm there."

"How do you get paid?" Aria asked.

"Direct deposit."

"So you really don't talk to him." Aria wasn't asking this time. She did seem sort of stunned though.

Farrah shook her head, her stomach starting to cramp from all the punch.

"But you will," Michelle said. "When you're ready to get back together with him."

"Michelle," Meredith warned.

"What? You don't think they'll get back together?" She looked at Meredith with challenge and then switched her gaze to Cheryl. "I've seen them together. Heck, we all have, right? They love each other." She drained the last of her punch, and Farrah wondered if hers wasn't spiked with something stronger than almond extract. "Of course they'll get back together."

"I...I think he's probably moved on," Farrah said. The words made her chest feel too small to house her heart. "I don't think he'll take me back."

"Why not?" Meredith asked, her curiosity open now.

The door opened and Audra and Meagan entered. Farrah thought maybe she'd be saved from answering, but Hazel waved them over and said, "Farrah's telling us about Darren."

"No, I—"

"He asked about you today," Meagan said, cutting her off. She wore a glint of excitement in her eyes.

"What did he say?" Aria asked, as if Darren were her ex-boyfriend.

"He just wanted to know how you felt things were going in the boutique. I said you hadn't mentioned anything one way or the other, and that I'd find out."

Farrah didn't like the weight of all the eyes that swiveled her way. "The boutique is fine."

Audra rolled her eyes, and Farrah's defenses shot up. "What? The boutique *is* fine. You're there every day. Do I complain about anything?"

"Sure, the boutique is fine. You're fine. Darren's *fine*." Audra set her purse down and reached for a cup. "But fine isn't a great way to live."

"That's because you're dating Sherwin," Farrah said, cocking her own eyebrows.

The women rounded on Audra now. "You're dating Sherwin?" Meagan practically screeched. "Sherwin Mayfair? Why didn't I know this?"

A healthy blush crawled across Audra's face. She looked at Farrah with murder and happiness in her eyes. "We—we're not really dating."

"I saw them kissing earlier this week," Farrah said. "The thing about a greenhouse is there's a lot of glass panels." She laughed, along with a couple of the other women.

"Fine." Audra lifted her chin. "I like Sherwin Mayfair, and we're dating."

Questions started, and she answered, and Farrah slipped to the back of the crowd, glad the spotlight was off her for a few minutes.

Meagan sidled over to her, her gaze still fixed on Audra. "You will go back to him, won't you?"

"I don't know, Meagan. I honestly don't think he'll take me back." She hadn't told anyone that she'd told Darren it wasn't his turn to star in her life. The more she thought about it, the more ridiculous it sounded. No wonder he'd worn his agony in his eyes, his jaw, his tone.

"Oh, honey. He's just waiting for you."

"Waiting for me to what?"

"Waiting for you to admit that you'd rather be unhappy with him than happy with anything and anyone else." She moved away, leaving her riddles in Farrah's ears.

Unhappy with him…

Than happy with anyone else.

She was glad to be in the company of her friends tonight. Her question about hosting hadn't been answered, but no one had thrown her out yet. She could rent the library or a room at the senior citizen center if she needed to. Or she could use someone else's house and set everything up, order food, all of it. She didn't have to live here to be friends with these women.

"Let's get started!" Meredith called, and everyone headed over to the high table to get scorecards and pencils. Farrah joined them, her spirits lifting with the easy banter, the quick laughter, and the delicious Christmas cookies and dipped chocolates.

But phrases from that conversation wouldn't leave her mind.

They love each other.

Of course they'll get back together.

Farrah wanted to believe that Darren loved her. She was so close to liking herself that the idea was almost believable.

Almost.

CHAPTER
TWENTY-ONE

Darren spent mornings in the house. Painting a bedroom that held no furniture. Making breakfast and then lunch for himself. Cleaning a bathroom. Installing a ceiling fan. He took his lunch out to the barn and stable with him, and he did a little work there each day too.

He had two cowhands to exercise and feed the handful of horses that he'd bought with the property. Sometimes he'd saddle Paintbrush and take the horse for a walk down the snowpacked road.

Afternoons usually found him out in the orchards. He didn't have a lot to do with the trees in the winter, but he liked their skeletal branches and he wanted to keep his eye on his new maple saplings.

Once Farrah left, he checked on the boutique, making good mental notes about how the fish were doing, and the progress of the plants. He'd been surprised at how easily this place maintained itself, but he also knew Farrah and Audra and Meagan—who hadn't quit yet—did an enormous amount of work he didn't even know about.

But the boutique didn't require much in terms of money, besides the occasional repair, which he could do himself.

In the evenings, after everyone had left the farm but him, he went out into one of the sheds in the backyard. Jim had once been a woodworker, and he'd left all his tools and machinery. Darren was slowly building himself a kitchen table, but he suspected the chairs would be too complex for his budding habit.

He watched videos online and he subscribed to a website that sent how-to tutorials to his email inbox. His hands found an easy rhythm with wood, and he felt certain that he'd be able to make beds and rocking chairs, couches and end tables, given enough time.

The scent of wood and shavings soothed him almost as much as riding Paintbrush or going to church. He hadn't been into town on the Sabbath since he'd purchased the farm. It was a fifteen minute drive, and he craved his solitude.

Still, as Christmas approached, he felt called to go hear what Pastor Gray had to say about the Savior. Maybe then he could close this year up right. Find a measure of peace to hold onto. Discover a way to be happier in the coming year.

He stepped through the doors of the church the Sunday before Christmas to a mob of people. He'd forgotten how busy the building could get during the holidays. Ben had saved him a sliver of space on the end of the row, and Darren folded himself into it.

"Merry Christmas," Ben said, beaming at him. "Rae wants you to come for dinner this afternoon since you'll be gone on Christmas Day."

"I suppose I can be persuaded," Darren said, grinning back. "Is she feeling better?" He looked past Ben to Rae, who sat with her hand on her very pregnant belly.

She seemed a bit flushed, but she said, "I'm fine, Darren. Bring yourself and maybe some of those oatmeal cookies Ben has been telling me about."

"You told her about my cookies?" Darren's mock horror made Ben chuckle.

"No raisins," Rae added just as the prelude music started.

Darren would never pollute an oatmeal cookie with raisins. At this point, he hoped he could make them edible. He'd never made them *for* anyone before, and he'd tasted Rae's baking. His cookies definitely weren't up to par. Most of the time he ate the dough instead of baking them into cookies.

Pastor Gray stood at the pulpit, his face practically glowing with heavenly light. He told the story of the Christ child's birth, and Darren sat back and relaxed. He could almost substitute his mother's voice in place of the pastor's. She loved the shepherds, and therefore, Darren had grown to love them too.

He hadn't thought of his mother quite so much as he had in the past couple of months. He'd brought his set of green napkins, embroidered with that B, to the farmhouse he was slowly making his. He'd been thinking about what it meant to be a Buttars.

And while he still wasn't entirely sure, he knew he wanted to live a good life, the way the Savior had.

"He focused on serving others," Pastor Gray said. "He never deviated from that. And we shouldn't either. Sometimes it can be hard to find ways to serve. Sometimes people resist the help. Pray, and God will put you where you're needed most."

He continued speaking about the miracles Jesus has performed while on the earth, and then he sat down in favor of letting the choir bring a spirit of peace and joy with several Christmas hymns.

The entire congregation stood and sang *Silent Night*, and the service ended. Darren hugged Rae and Ben and tried to get out before the exits got too clogged. He didn't let his head swivel to find Farrah.

In reality, he could see her anytime he wanted. All he had to do was walk out to the botanical boutique. He never did, wanting to give her what he'd promised he would. He made it to his truck without incident, but his feet froze to the pavement when he saw a bright red envelope stuck under his windshield wiper. The festive paper flapped in the wind, and Darren glanced around to see if anyone was watching him.

Satisfied they weren't, he hurried toward the bright spot of color in the winter landscape and pulled it from under the wiper blade. No name. No handwriting at all.

He climbed into the truck and stared it, gripping the thin envelope in his fingers. Not wanting to get stuck in the parking lot once everyone started leaving, he pulled onto the road and headed away from the church.

After a few blocks, he pulled over and looked at the item that had been left on his truck. He slid his finger under the sealed flap and broke it. An invitation lay inside, easily recognizable by the thick paper and bold lettering that read "Housewarming Party" across the top.

He withdrew the invitation completely, his eyes eating up the information on it.

"Farrah moved?" He flipped the invitation to the other side, but it was blank. The address on the front was in Burlington.

Darren gasped as if he'd been kicked square in the chest by a horse.

She'd moved. She was gone.

And she'd told him by placing an invitation to her housewarming party on his truck during the Sunday service?

He wasn't sure what to think, but he knew he hated holding that glossy paper as if he was supposed to be happy she now lived a half an hour away. Like he would be buying her a houseplant and showing up to her ridiculous party.

The familiar anger he'd experienced most of the summer raced through him. If he came face-to-face with Farrah, they'd probably argue like they had before getting back together this past fall.

He was so tired of arguing. With her. With himself.

So he'd fallen for her.

He could pick himself up and move on. He could. He *would*. He just needed to figure out how.

One more glance at that invitation, and it looked like she'd moved on without him, literally. He kept telling himself it didn't matter. They weren't together. She could do whatever she wanted.

He arrived at his farm, and went through the motions of making oatmeal cookies. The house filled with the scent of warm brown sugar, and Darren texted Sam and Logan while the first batch of cookies baked.

Texts came pouring in, mostly from Logan. He and Layla were more excited about Darren's visit to California the following day than Darren was. He smiled at the exuberance in his brother's texts, and the thought of eating lunch on the beach—as Logan had promised—sounded amazing.

While the second tray of cookies baked, he collected the presents he'd bought for Ben and Rae and his new friends and employees of the farm. He'd meant to get the gifts out to everyone earlier, but he hadn't wanted to run into Farrah. Silly, probably. He had a carefully wrapped box for her. Of course he was going to have to see her.

But no, he'd planned on leaving it in the boutique, where she'd find it and open it in private. The gift wasn't anything special. A box of purple dice he'd bought online, and a package of pencils decorated with vines. He'd heard through Rae that Farrah had joined the bunko group permanently, and he was glad she'd started making friends. He took that as a good sign in her well-being.

Now, he looked at the box, a skiff of foolishness racing

down his spine. She'd moved away from Island Park. Maybe she wouldn't be doing bunko here next year. Maybe she'd quit her job in the boutique and she hadn't told him yet.

His heart pounded, and he thought about calling her. Just to ask. Just to say *Merry Christmas* since he wouldn't be here on Tuesday. Maybe see if she wanted to come to Ben's—

He cut off his thoughts, which could derail so easily when it came to Farrah. *No*, he told himself. *She'll come to you when she's ready to deal with you.*

He hated that he was "something to be dealt with." The timer went off on the batch of cookies, and Darren gripped the hot pad to get the tray out of the oven. Maybe she'd already come to him. She'd left that invitation on his windshield. Was that an invitation to her party? Or back into her life?

Confused and exhausted with his mental war, he took a deep breath. "It's almost Christmas," he said aloud to the house. "Can't I get a moment of peace on Christmas?" He tipped his head toward the ceiling and added, "Please?"

Nothing much happened, other than some of the tension drained from Darren's shoulders. He sighed and picked up a freshly baked cookie. The melted chocolate and crisp edges made him moan. He could definitely take these to Rae's for dinner and not be embarrassed.

He could run by Sherwin Mayfair's to deliver his gift. Darren hadn't known what to get the man who'd been essentially running the farm. Sherwin took care of the livestock, the schedule for planting, the equipment, all of it.

Jim had been focused on the orchards, and he had spent most of his time there.

Darren had relied on Sherwin to learn the ropes of this farm, and he'd asked the man if they could meet after the new year to properly rename the farm.

Sherwin lived in town, and he'd started dating Audra a couple of months ago. At a loss for what he might like, Darren had written him a note and added some cash to the envelope. He'd never been a boss before, and he wasn't sure what protocol was. He wasn't sure he cared what protocol was.

While the cookies cooled, he took his gifts out to his truck. He'd stop by Sherwin's and Audra's, Callie's and Carlson's. That was his whole staff—*don't forget about Farrah*—and they all seemed to get along great.

And how could he forget about Farrah? Her box mocked him, still sitting on the end table he'd finished last week. Should he put it with the others? Stop by her place as he was out?

Surely she wouldn't be there. She'd probably gone to her parents' house, especially now that they lived in the same town.

"One way to find out," he said, marching over to the box and picking it up. He put it with the others in the truck and returned to the house for the cookies. With three paper plates stacked with still-warm cookies, he headed out the front door one more time.

"Oh!" a woman cried out as he barreled straight into her.

He fumbled, grunted, couldn't find a handhold. The

cookies tumbled to the ground. He held his hands out to his sides as he stared in disbelief at the mess on the porch. Slowly, he lifted his eyes to the woman.

"Farrah?" he asked.

"I'm so sorry." She dropped to her knees and started swiping cookies off the ground. "These are still warm."

Darren stared at her for a few seconds before his brain kicked back into gear. He bent to retrieve the cookies too. They gathered them all, slight wisps of steam from the cookies lifting into the chilly air.

She held one plate while he balanced two. After wiping a lock of her hair off her forehead, she looked at him.

Darren's chest ached with the beautiful lines of her face. The softness he found in her eyes. So much about her had changed, and yet everything was still the same.

"What are you doin' here?" he asked.

CHAPTER
TWENTY-TWO

Farrah liked the throaty, hoarse quality of Darren's voice. The dark, warm depths of his eyes. The way he sat by his brother at church. His determination and hard-working spirit.

She wasn't sure how close to whole she was, but she knew she liked herself more each day. She knew she wanted Darren in her life again. By the soft, adoring look in his eyes, maybe he'd forgive her. Take her back. Maybe they could work through their problems and find a way to be together.

With those heavy thoughts in her mind, she cleared her throat. "It's almost Christmas," she said, backing up a step. "I didn't want—well, I came to check on the new mushrooms, and I saw your truck here, and I didn't want…you to be alone…today." For some reason she couldn't name.

Coolness entered those eyes. "I'm going to Ben's for

dinner. They asked me to bring the dessert." He indicated the cookies.

"When did you learn how to bake?"

"'Bout the time I started livin' on my own."

His tone cut through her, and Farrah gave a few quick bursts of a nod. "Okay, well, I'm glad to know you won't be alone." She handed him the paper plate. "Merry Christmas, Darren."

She'd taken three steps when he said, "Wait."

Farrah's insides quivered with hope. She turned and tucked her hair behind her ear. She wasn't sure if the damage she'd done to Darren could ever be repaired. She had spoken true when she said she'd come to check the mushrooms and seen his truck. And she didn't want him to be alone.

For so long, she hadn't trusted herself or how she felt. She hadn't known who she was. But she did now.

"I'm moving to Burlington," she said when he remained silent. "Did you get my invitation to the party?"

"Yes." His jaw tightened, and everything she needed to know about how he felt passed between them. "Why are you moving up there?"

"I'm starting school at the University of Vermont in January." Pride lilted in her voice. "I'm going to finish my agribusiness degree."

His muscles released and a quick smile graced his handsome face. "That's great, Farrah." His voice caught on her name, and the dam she'd collected her emotions behind cracked.

She'd needed to talk to him for weeks about her school

schedule affecting her job. But now she needed to talk to him about something more important. So she gathered her courage close. Closer.

"The party's next weekend. I'm not moving until next Thursday." And she needed a truck. And a couple of really strong arms. "Might you be available to help me move?" She gestured to his truck. "And can I borrow your truck?"

He took a step closer, his eyes blazing with heat now. She wasn't sure if it was the desirable kind or the angry kind. Maybe both.

"Using me for my truck, is that it?" His playfulness sent love straight to her heart, puncturing all the worry she held there.

She lifted one shoulder in what she hoped was a flirtatious shrug. "And your muscles."

He reached past her and balanced the plates of cookies on the porch railing. "Farrah." His voice could paint beautiful pictures, especially when whispered with so much emotion. His hand brushed hers. "I'm—"

"I only sent one invitation," she blurted, suddenly needing to lay all her cards on the table before he rejected her. Or told her he was worried about her. Or said something to put more distance between them.

"For the housewarming party." She lifted her eyes and stared straight into his. "I only gave out one invitation." Her lungs shook as she drew in a cold breath of air. "I really hope he'll come. Otherwise, it'll just be me and a bunch of food." She giggled, pulling it back when it sounded manic in her own ears.

Darren inched closer. "What kind of food?" He leaned

down and inhaled her hair as he swept both arms around her. "Because I'm allergic to blueberries. I don't think I ever told you that."

Farrah melted into his embrace, resting her cheek against his pulse. Everything she'd ever been worried about seemed to evaporate, and she wanted to stay in this moment forever. "No, you never told me that," she confirmed.

"Do you have time to help me deliver presents?" he whispered. "I meant to get them out sooner, but…I didn't."

"Presents for who?" Her brain felt the teensiest bit soft, probably because she'd been expecting a fight from Darren, not pure acceptance and forgiveness.

"The farm people. You know, Sherwin, Audra, Cassie, Carlson." He pulled back, stepped away, shoved his hands in his pockets, and dipped his chin so his cowboy hat hid his eyes. "You."

Her heart started beating irregularly.

"It's nothing special," he drawled. "So don't get too excited."

No matter what it was, Farrah suspected he'd lost sleep over thinking about it. Probably had for everyone on his staff at his new farm. "I can help," she said. "My mom's serving dinner at four."

"Just the three of you?"

"And a few people from their church who don't have family in the area."

Darren nodded and lifted his head. "All the presents are in the truck. Want to ride with me? Or you could park at the sports complex and we can go from there."

"What time do you need to get to Rae's?"

"I don't know."

"You didn't ask her when dinner was?"

"Ben said this afternoon."

"So we have time to go together." She watched Darren swallow, then nod. He gestured for her to go down the steps first, and the thunk of his cowboy boots behind her brought such a smile to her face.

She went to the driver's side door and waited for him to reach past her to open it. Feeling brave, and bold, and like maybe she had finally found the last piece of the puzzle she needed to truly like herself, she grabbed his hand as he pulled it back.

Twisting toward him, she said, "I've really missed you."

Darren blinked at her, his lips parting into a soft smile that faded quickly. "Farrah, I—well, we have a lot to talk about."

"Doesn't have to be today," she said. "Maybe we can just spend some time together."

"I don't love you," he said, his words rushed and harsh when they landed in her ears.

Her insides iced. "Oh." Of course he didn't. And how naïve and foolish had she been to believe he still did, after all this time? After months of silence? After she'd told him it *wasn't his turn*?

Those words still haunted her in her lowest moments, and she worked not to sink into that darkness now.

"I will again," he said. "I know that. But it won't be the same."

She wasn't sure what he was saying. By the squint of his eyes and the line between his eyebrows, he looked like maybe he wasn't sure what he was saying either.

Farrah turned away, something stinging in her chest she couldn't get to stop.

"It will be better," he said, tugging her back around. He gazed at her with all the love and adoration she'd dreamt about. "Can I kiss you now, Farrah?" He lifted one hand and trailed his fingers down the side of her face, along her neck above the collar of her coat.

She shook her head. "I'm—I didn't come here to kiss you."

"You don't want to?"

Oh, she did. Badly. She licked her lips and swallowed. Her mouth felt cold from the Vermont winter air, and she couldn't stop herself from nodding. "I want to." Her words whisped into the air and hung there, the same way the white clouds of her breath did. "I just need—I want—I think we should talk first."

"All right." He waited for her to climb into the truck. She had to push several boxes, packages, and bags to the side to make room. Then he handed her the plates of cookies and got in beside her.

He said nothing on the drive to town, and the silence between them was so comfortable that Farrah didn't want to break it.

Darren did with, "I'm going to California tomorrow for Christmas. I'll be gone all week."

"Sounds fun," Farrah said, though going to California was on her list of things never to do again. "I'm staying with my parents tonight, and I'll be back in the afternoon to check on the boutique."

He turned down Rooster Avenue and pulled into a driveway that ended at a red brick house. "Did you want to come?"

She shook her head. "You go on."

"This is Sherwin." He glanced across her lap. "There should be a blue envelope…."

Farrah plucked it from under a red-wrapped box and handed it to Darren. "When you get back, I want to talk to you about my schedule at the farm."

Surprise passed through his expression. "Of course. We can work out whatever you need."

Gratitude filled her, and she watched him walk through the winter weather to Sherwin's front door. He turned back a moment later and jogged back to the passenger side of the truck. "Audra's here, so I need her gift too." He dug through the pile on the seat and selected a bag covered in blue snowmen. "Be right back."

He'd never answered her about helping with the move or lending her his truck. *Thank you for the courage to talk to Darren*, she thought.

When he returned, she told him about her morning classes, and how she'd like to come to the farm at eleven, and stay until seven. "I'll work through lunch," she said. "I promise I won't fall behind."

"Whatever you need, Farrah," he said, setting the truck toward the south edge of town now. "I know you'll get the job done." He pulled into another driveway and put the truck in park. "I'm not worried about it."

"Thanks." She wanted to lean into his shoulder, twine her fingers with his. Instead, she handed him the package he requested and maintained her position in the truck while he went up to Carlson's door.

After he delivered Cassie's gift, he said, "Well, that one's for you." He nodded toward the box wrapped in red and white striped paper. It was about the size of a shoebox, and when she picked it up, the contents slid from one end to the other.

"It's pretty lame," he said, his voice gruff. "You can open it later."

"Whatever. I don't want to open it later." She pulled off the end of the paper and saw a shoebox inside. Upon opening that, she found a clear plastic box of purple dice. A squeal sounded from her throat.

She yanked the dice out of the box and shook them. "Is this for bunko night?"

"Rae said you joined the group permanently."

"I did." She laughed, and it felt so good. "Thank you, Darren." She reached in and pulled out a package of pencils with green vines all over them. "And what's bunko night without the cutest pencils to keep score with?"

He grunted and kept driving. She noticed he'd taken the turn toward Steeple Ridge, but she didn't say anything. Her giddiness over his gifts wouldn't allow anything to ruin this moment.

"Thank you, Darren." She stretched up to kiss him on the cheek, and then she looked at her designer dice again. She could definitely plan something to go with the purple dice when it was her month to host. Purple foods, purple decorations.... Her mind spun with the possibilities.

Darren pulled into the public parking lot at Steeple Ridge. "We've got hours until dinner," he said. "Want to ride?"

A sense of peace filled her. "Yeah, I'd like that." She got her horse saddled, and she and Darren set out on a worn path in the snow.

"So are you still seeing Doctor Kenna?" he asked.

"No." Farrah squirmed in her saddle. "I stopped seeing her just before Thanksgiving. She...wasn't helping."

"What did help?"

Farrah let several strides of the horse go by as she thought about the past several months. "Learning to trust how I feel," she said. "And relying on the Lord, not what someone else said, or did, or thought." She glanced over at him and saw a strong, patient man who had figured that out long ago.

"I'm glad, Farrah."

She was too, and she tilted her face toward the sun, trying to soak up all the warmth she could. She was glad she'd stopped trying to please Dr. Kenna. Glad she'd stopped second-guessing herself. Glad she'd learned to rely on God.

Glad she was here, on this farm, with Darren. Though he rode his brother's horse, he belonged on a farm like this one. And Farrah realized she did too.

"So what are you going to name your farm?" she asked as they approached the tree line.

He exhaled, as if the topic had been weighing him

down. "I think I'm going to stick with what the Bybee's started. I'll just change Bybee to Buttars."

"Buttars Botanical Farm," she said, a smile spreading her lips. "I like that."

"Yeah, me too," he said. "My mother always told me it means something to be a Buttars, so I better be a good one. Might as well drive by that sign everyday to remind myself of that."

"I would've liked to have met your mother," Farrah said, the words barely leaving her mouth loud enough to be heard.

"I would've liked that too." Darren met her eye, and though they still had leagues to go to unpack everything between them, Farrah saw the love in his eyes. She hoped it was shining in hers too.

CHAPTER
TWENTY-THREE

On Christmas Eve, Darren touched down in California to golden sunshine and a blue sky. For some reason, he still expected the breathtaking cold to enter his lungs when he stepped out of the airport at Long Beach. It didn't come, but Layla's squeal and Logan's laughter did.

Darren embraced them both and had only taken one step when Logan said, "Farrah showed up yesterday?"

He nodded, a smile coming to his soul though he tried not to be too giddy. But he'd been happier since he'd nearly trampled her yesterday than he had been in a while. He'd told Ben and Rae about it, and then texted Logan right before he'd gone to bed.

He'd lain there for a while, staring up into the darkness, begging God to guide him when it came to Farrah. Give him patience. Compassion. Understanding.

"Well, what did she say?" Logan asked. "We've been dyin' out here, waiting for you to arrive."

Darren tossed his bag in the back of Logan's truck. "She apologized." He looked at his brother and sister-in-law. They'd always supported him, talked with him when he needed it. Heck, it was Layla who had matched him with Farrah. "We're talking."

"That's it?" Layla's eyebrows rose. "She didn't say she wanted to get back together or anything?"

"She asked me to help her move, and she invited me to her housewarming party." Darren waited for her to climb in and slide into the middle of the bench seat. He got in beside her. "She only invited me to the party. I guess I'll have to go."

Layla slugged him in the bicep and he chuckled. "Seriously, guys, it's no big deal."

Logan snorted. "No big deal. He says it's no big deal, Lay. I totally believe him. Don't you?" His brother's sarcasm coated the cab.

"Oh, yeah," Layla said, laying it on thick too. "He's not freaking out or anything."

"I'm not," Darren said. "It's going to be...different this time."

"How so?" Logan asked, pulling onto the busiest freeway Darren had ever seen. He gripped the armrest and marveled that his brother knew how to navigate this kind of traffic.

"For one, we're not fighting."

"Mm hm," Layla said.

"No, really. We didn't at all. We just drove around

and talked, and then we rode until it was time for dinner." It had pretty much been the most perfect afternoon Darren had ever experienced, and he hoped he could remember the comfortable hours he'd spent with Farrah forever.

"We barely touched, and well." He cleared his throat. "She wouldn't let me kiss her."

"Goin' slow," Logan said. "That's probably smart."

Darren's brain thought so. His heart wanted to press on the accelerator, the same way it had this summer. But he hated how that segment of their relationship had ended, and he wasn't willing to repeat it.

So if he needed to go slow, as if they'd just met and were getting to know each other, he would.

"I just realized something," he blurted.

"What?" Logan and Layla said together.

"I have to get to know her again," he said. "She's not the same woman I met last fall. Or the one I dated this summer. She's...changed."

"So have you," Layla said, grinning at him.

"I have?"

"Sure," she said. "You talk more, for one. And you smile more. And you bought a farm and have a completely different life now than you did last fall."

"So we're basically starting over." Darren thought he'd care more than he did. He didn't need to get married right away.

"You're coming home, too," Layla said. "You two belong together. You'll find your way home together." She sighed happily and hooked her arm through Darren's.

"Now, I hope you brought your swim trunks, because we're eating dinner on the beach."

DARREN'S SYSTEM FELT LIKE IT WAS ON A YO-YO. COLD, warm, cold. He'd been back in Vermont for three days, but he'd returned to a warm house. Then gone out to cold Steeple Ridge to ride and collect Rambo from the cowboys that had taken care of him while Darren was away.

Back to the warmth of the fireplace, to Rambo sleeping on his feet at night, to hot coffee in the mornings.

But not this morning.

This morning, he was clapping his hands together to keep them warm while he loaded Farrah's boxes into the back of his truck. She was organized in a purely chaotic event. Each box had been packed, taped, and labeled. All he had to do was go in, grab them, take them out, load them up.

He went from warm, to cold, and back to warm.

By the time she got back with the rental truck, only her furniture remained. "Sorry," she said as she climbed down from the cab. "They wanted to give me this giant one, and said they didn't have this sized one, and it took forever." She swiped her hair off her forehead and flashed him a flustered smile.

"But this is the one you want?" He reached to lift the sliding door in the back.

"Yeah, it should fit everything. I don't have that much."

He peered at her. "Farrah, the house is full of furniture."

"Oh, but I'm not taking it all," she said, striding back toward the house. "I marked the things I'm taking with an orange tag."

Darren walked through the house with her, and sure enough, with only a bed, the dresser, two couches, and her dining set, she wasn't taking everything.

"What are you doing with the rest of this?" he asked. The spare bedroom held furniture she hadn't tagged. End tables in the living room. A dish cabinet in the kitchen. Her patio furniture in her beautiful backyard.

"Meredith and Denny said I could leave anything I wanted," Farrah said. "They're moving from a condo, so they don't have rooms of furniture. I'm moving to a condo, so I don't need rooms of furniture." She glanced around her house, her expression taking on a wistful quality.

"You're not having second thoughts about moving, are you?" He lifted two dining chairs and paused.

"No," she said, yanking her attention back to him. "No, it's only fifteen minutes from the farm, and miles closer to school. I just…I will miss my yard." She stepped toward him and he set the chairs down to receive her into his embrace.

"You have the farm," he whispered. "You can do my yard work any time you want."

She curled into his chest and sighed. "I do love the farm."

"You can plant anything you want out there," he said. "Choose any spot, Farrah. It's yours." He couldn't help the emotion in his words. They had gone slow. He'd been back in town for four days, and he hadn't texted her until this morning. But he liked this soft, strong, sexy person Farrah had become. He liked that she shared important things with him. That she had dreams and was working to achieve them.

"Thank you, Darren." She stepped away and met his gaze. Reaching up, she cupped his face in her palm. "Thank you."

He gazed back at her, and he liked what he saw. "I like you," he whispered. "Can we go to dinner in Burlington once we get you moved and settled?"

"You like me?"

He could've said dozens of things to emphasize how much. Instead, he just said, "Yes."

Half a smile flirted with her lips. "I like me too."

"I'm glad."

"And you too. I like you too."

Feeling a bit insane and with his heart pressing on the accelerator, he bent down and skated his lips along her cheek. "So let's get you moved."

THE HOUSEWARMING PARTY STARTED AT SIX O'CLOCK, AND Darren arrived several hours early. He'd spent Thursday night at dinner with her and followed her home on Friday after her work in the boutique.

One piece at a time, everything was getting unpacked between them. So on Saturday, he couldn't stand to wait all day to see her. They'd held hands, and laid together on the couch to watch a movie, and shared meals and stories with each other.

He wanted to kiss her.

And today happened to be New Year's Eve. Whether she'd planned her housewarming party on this holiday or not, Darren wasn't sure.

He texted her from the parking lot, so when he knocked on her door, she was laughing when she opened it. She wore yoga pants and a blue T-shirt. Her hair looked like she hadn't washed it yet, but Darren found her downright beautiful.

"Sorry I'm early." He stepped past her and entered her condo. "You can do whatever you need to. I'll just hang out."

She scoffed and closed the door behind him. "Right. If you're here, you're going to work." She latched onto his hand and pulled him into the kitchen. "I'm doing barbeque chicken tonight, and it needs to marinate." She glanced over her shoulder. "Then you can take me to lunch. I found a salad bar next to campus I want to try."

He stood in the kitchen like he didn't know what any of the tools were. Really, he'd been cooking for himself since he moved to the farm, and he'd become quite adept at putting together a meal.

So he got to work measuring and cutting and putting the chicken in the Crock Pot. Farrah made baked beans and told him about the campus she'd visited while he was in California. He listened and asked her questions. Took her to lunch. Laughed with her when he stepped in an icy puddle and soaked his boots.

Back at her place, he kicked off his shoes and socks so they could dry. They watched a movie in the afternoon, and when six o'clock rolled around, Darren was fast asleep.

CHAPTER
TWENTY-FOUR

Farrah watched Darren sleep, his face the most handsome thing she'd ever seen. She gently traced her fingers along his hairline, her huge emotions for him engulfing her.

"I love you, Darren," she whispered.

He didn't twitch, and Farrah wanted many more days and evenings like this one with him. She'd been dreaming of a midnight New Year's kiss with him, a way to start their new life together, the perfect beginning to a year she hoped would be spent with him.

But she couldn't wait six more hours. She shifted on the couch, which caused him to move too. He groaned and his hand against her waist tightened as he pulled her closer to him, almost unconsciously.

"Darren?" she whispered.

He was sleepy and his eyes didn't open when he said, "Mm?"

She touched her lips to his, the warmth from his body searing into hers. He woke, his kiss becoming firmer before softening again. He kissed her and kissed her in that slow, passionate way he had. But this time it was completely different.

It was like the first time all over again, because Farrah was a completely different person who needed to experience her first kiss with a beautiful man.

"That was the best way to wake up," he murmured against her lips before claiming them again. He finally ended the kiss and his eyes drifted open. "Farrah, I know we have a long way to go still, but I lied to you earlier. I'm still in love with you. I can't seem to stop loving you, even when I try."

She smiled and placed a kiss on the corner of his eye. Left, then right. "I love you too, Darren."

She'd never said those words out loud, and emotions streamed across his face. "Yeah?"

"Yeah." She giggled and trailed her fingertips over his earlobe. "I want to be a Buttars. I've heard it means something, and I think I could be a pretty good one."

"The best," he whispered.

"You think so?"

"I think you've been working really hard at a lot of things." He stroked his hand down her hair once, then twice. "Working hard at being the best person you know how to be. So yeah, I think you'd be a terrific Buttars."

"When do you want to make that happen?"

"Are you askin' me to marry you?"

She giggled and tucked her face into the crook of his

neck. The scent of his skin, so much like musk and leather and fresh cotton, prompted her to draw in a deep breath. "No." She snuggled closer though that was hard to do. "I'm asking when you're going to ask me to marry you."

His chest lifted and then went down as he exhaled. "Oh, I don't know, Farrah. I don't even have a ring yet." He rubbed slow circles on her back with his fingers, making her whole body tingle.

"I'll admit that I haven't thought about my wedding much."

"Good." He sat up, pushing her gently off him as he did. "That way, you won't be disappointed when it's just me and you and Pastor Gray."

She tucked her hair behind her ear and stared at him. "What about your brothers? That cute baby you go on and on about?"

He chuckled. So maybe baby Jackie had smitten him over Thanksgiving weekend. "Fine, they can all come too." He lifted her fingers to his lips and kissed each one on her right hand.

"And my bunko friends? And my parents, of course. And I might meet some friends at school. And Tucker and Missy—"

"All right, all right." Darren chuckled and pulled her to him for another kiss. "We can invite everyone." He held her close, both hands around the back of her neck. "And I'll ask you properly, okay? I don't know how or when, but that'll come."

She nodded, a flush rising through her core and into

her face. "So should we eat? The party was supposed to begin fifteen minutes ago."

"I'm starving." But he barely let her stand before taking her into his arms and kissing her again.

SEVERAL WEEKS LATER, FARRAH FINALLY FELT LIKE SHE'D found a rhythm to her life. She got up early and did homework before class. She rushed from her permaculture class to the salad shop to the boutique. Her work there kept her busy, and though Audra had taken over all the delivery and sales of the produce they grew, Farrah still felt like she was constantly behind.

Darren arrived in the boutique by six-forty-five each evening and watched her work. Asked her questions about her classes, the strawberries, the varieties of lettuce. At seven o'clock, he led her back to his house with his hand in hers.

He always had dinner ready, or he'd driven to town to pick something up. Rambo greeted her with a single bark and a quick lick on her hand. She relaxed in their company, exclaiming over any new piece of furniture Darren had completed or started. He had a way with wood, and by the time March dawned, he'd completed the new sign for his farm.

He took her out to his woodshop to see it, hanging back as she stepped over to the giant sign on the work table.

"Wow." She traced her fingers along the top of the sign, where he'd carved big letters to spell out his last name.

He'd painted them bright yellow, like sunflowers. The joyfulness of the color made her smile. "This is gorgeous."

He'd carved in flowers and trees as well, all of them painted in bright colors. The words "Botanical Farm" sat in a single line beneath his last name, and the whole thing spanned a good six feet.

He came up beside her and gazed down at the sign. "Too bright?"

"No, it's going to be perfect out on that road." She glanced at him. "Just perfect."

He hadn't asked her to marry him yet, and she had no indication that he'd even thought about it again. He hadn't mentioned it, or brought up a wedding ring, nothing. Farrah had followed his lead and kept her mouth shut.

She was enjoying college, and she had just gotten settled enough to consider adding something else to her to-do list. Maybe that was how he felt too.

"How are things on the farm?" she asked as he laced his fingers through hers.

"Going great. Our sugar maples aren't going to sap this year, but they're on track for next April."

"Are you going to hang tea lights in them?" She went with him as he took her to the couch in the corner and sat down.

"Should I?" He lifted his arm over her shoulders.

"There's a big sugar maple park in Montpelier," she said. "That's what they do. It's very romantic."

"I'll look into that."

But he didn't need to. Darren was romantic in dozens of ways, from how he sometimes texted her to say, *I was in town and bought you a berry nut salad so you don't need to stop after class today.*

He put it on the desk in the boutique so it was waiting for her. He saddled her a horse when she wanted to go riding. He provided dinner and company for her every evening. He let her talk as much or as little as she wanted.

"My bathroom sink is still leaking," she said with a sigh as she leaned into him.

"I'll come on Saturday." His voice sounded sleepy, and sure enough, a few moments later, he yawned. "Oh, hey, I have something for you in the kitchen."

"You do?" They'd just finished dinner, and they'd cleaned up in the kitchen together. She hadn't seen anything out of the ordinary.

His eyes glittered like dark diamonds as he nodded. "I'm, well, it's…. Maybe we should just go see." He rose to his feet, and she went with him.

Once in the kitchen, her eyes swept the familiar space. He hadn't done anything to remodel, but the dark cabinets were beautiful. The countertops were in good shape. The floor had been replaced recently, but Darren hadn't done it.

Everything looked as it had a half an hour ago. Clean. Wiped down. Everything put in its place. Quintessential Darren.

"I don't get it," she said, glancing around, her heartbeat increasing like maybe something would pop out at her and startle her.

"Rambo probably ran off with it. Just a sec." Darren released her hand and stepped to the doorway that led into the dining room. He whistled and called, "Rambo! C'mon boy. Where you at?"

The dog's claws clicked on the hardwood as he came trotting over to Darren. "There you are. Did you take Farrah's present?" He scrubbed the dog's ears affectionately. "Go on. Go give it to her."

Rambo came over, and Farrah caught sight of something in his mouth. It looked black, and she stooped to try to get it out from between his teeth.

Darren leaned against the counter and said, "Drop it, Rambo."

The dog dropped a black jewelry box on the floor. Before Farrah could even move, Darren retrieved it. He cracked the box open to reveal a bright, shiny diamond, and she straightened slowly, her eyes never leaving the gem.

"You said you wanted to be a Buttars," he said.

Farrah lifted her eyes to his, her breath frozen in her lungs. "I do."

A smile graced his face. "And I'd like to spend my life with you. I've got this great big house, and it needs to be filled with more than me. So? What do you think? Will you marry me?"

He didn't even need to ask, but Farrah loved that he did, almost like she might say no. Warmth glowed in her chest, and she returned his smile. "Yes, Darren. I'll marry you."

He removed the ring from the box and slipped it on her finger. She giggled and he laughed, and then he sobered long enough to kiss her like he was her fiancé.

"When do you think you'd like to get married?" he asked. "Like, maybe next weekend?"

Her sigh turned into a choke. "Next weekend?"

"I'm dying here alone." He brushed his lips against her temple, down her cheek, and along her jawline. "This place needs a feminine touch, and I'm tired of watching you drive away at night."

She tipped her head back and let him trail a line of kisses up to her ear. "So…next weekend?"

She giggled and pushed fruitlessly against his chest. "What about June?" she asked. 'That gives me three months, and time to finish my semester, and I love Steeple Ridge in the summer."

He pulled back at the mention of his old farm. "Steeple Ridge?"

"I want to get married at Steeple Ridge. I think it would be like coming home."

"But this is our farm now." He watched her with a wary expression, and Farrah searched for the right explanation.

"The one time I thought about my wedding," she started. "I saw myself out at my favorite place—Steeple Ridge." She shrugged. "So if you don't care where we get married, I want to do it at Steeple Ridge."

"Steeple Ridge is fine with me, sweetheart." He inched his way toward her mouth. "Three months? June is a firm date for you?"

"Yes, June is firm," she whispered, her breath mingling with his just before he claimed her mouth in another kiss. Farrah kissed him back, her happiness shooting toward the stars at the very idea of becoming his wife in only three short months.

Read on for a sneak peek of **SECOND CHANCE RANCH**, Book 1 in the Three Rivers Ranch romance series!

Order it in ebook, paperback, or audiobook by scanning the QR code below.

SNEAK PEEK! SECOND CHANCE RANCH - CHAPTER 1

The walls in Kelly Russell's life had never seemed so close. Of course, they hadn't been this putrid shade of yellow for a long time, either. Her parents lived with the motto of "use it up, wear it out, make it do, or do without," and kitchen wall paint was no exception.

But if Kelly could ace this morning's job interview, she had a chance of getting her own walls again. Soon. And she'd paint them. Maybe blue, or purple, or green. Something cool. Anything but the stark white she'd had in California—or this dark yellow.

"I have to drive out to the ranch." She straightened her jacket as she glanced toward her mom and son, who sat at the kitchen table eating breakfast. She'd sailed through her college admissions interview in this jacket. She'd been hired for her first real job in this jacket. She'd also worn this jacket in divorce court and been granted full custody of her son, Finn.

She hoped the turquoise number would work its magic today. She tugged down the hemline, wondering when her black skirt had gotten a smidge too small.

Probably while you were sitting on the beach these past five years. She knew there'd be no sitting at Three Rivers Ranch, though she hoped the accountant would at least have an office.

"It's about twenty-five miles on that old, dirt road," she continued, knowing her four-year-old son wasn't listening, but hoping her mother was. "So I'll be gone for, I don't know, at least two hours. Maybe three."

"We'll be fine," her mom said. "I've taken care of children before."

"I know." Kelly pressed her lips together and determined that she did not need another layer of lipstick. She'd slick on clear gloss just before the interview. "But it's been a long time."

It had been twenty-four years, to be exact, since Kelly had been four. And her mother didn't seem as sharp as she once had.

Her dad grumped his way into the kitchen, but Kelly knew his frowny face was an act. "Hey, Finny," he said. "Want to go throw the pigskin?"

"Just a second, Daddy." Kelly crouched down and drew her son into a hug. "Love you, baby. Be good for Grandma and Grandpa."

She stood, and a sliver of nervous energy ran through her as she thought about returning to the ranch she'd loved as a teenager. She could practically smell the dust, hear the horses whinnying, and picture her best friend waving from the front porch, though Chelsea lived in Dallas now.

"Three Rivers needs a new financial controller," her mom said as she walked with Kelly to the front door. "You're qualified, and Frank knows you. He'd have to be dead not to hire you."

"Didn't you say he was going to be retiring soon?" Kelly worried the inside of her bottom lip with her teeth.

"That's what Glenda said." Mom put both hands on Kelly's shoulders as Kelly pictured the ladies down at the hair salon gossiping about everything from the price of beef to who'd moved in over the weekend. "You've got this." Her mom nodded and released her.

A rush of appreciation lifted Kelly's lips into a smile. "Thanks, Mom."

As she drove away from her childhood home, she made a mental list of things she could thank her parents for. Giving her a fabulous childhood under the wide, Texas sky. Paying for fifteen years of dance classes, which had provided her with a skill she'd used to fund her college education. Teaching her how to laugh.

Allowing her and Finn to take over their basement after her divorce.

She thought of her work at the local grocer as she pointed her pathetic excuse for a car toward the ranch. She'd been back in Three Rivers for several weeks, and she'd taken the first job she could get. But ringing up milk didn't pay well enough for her to buy her own house and raise a child. And the nearest dance studio was in Amarillo, fifty miles away. The investment of time and money to get there and back didn't make teaching ballet a viable option.

Kelly's fingers tightened on the steering wheel. "I've got this," she repeated. The gently rolling hills calmed her, as they always had. She'd spent countless hours out here with nothing but her thoughts, the wind, and her friends. The open, blue sky further anchored her. She'd loved lying on her back in Chelsea's backyard, creating stories from the clouds that rolled by. And the summer storms—she and Chelsea had made up their own songs, their own lyrics, their own choreography, all to the sound of thunder.

By the time she turned down the dirt driveway that led to the homestead, a sense of peace filled her. This ranch had been her second home growing up, and coming back to it now felt right. If she could get this job, it would be the first step toward getting her whole life back.

The nerves returned. She took a deep breath at the sight of the familiar house, imposing the first time you saw it. But Kelly knew better. She'd been in every room, felt the love and warmth from the family pictures hanging on the walls.

Kelly laughed at the memory at the same time her chest squeezed. Working at Three Rivers would provide a little safety at a time when Kelly had none. No pressure or anything.

She noted the American flag flying in the front yard of the ranch-style home. She'd kept in touch with Chelsea over the years and knew her younger brother, Squire, had joined the Army. His mother was obviously proud.

Kelly wondered if she'd get to see Heidi today, maybe experience one of her powder-scented hugs. A nostalgic smile played at her lips. She hoped so.

She left the house behind as she drove to the edge of the homestead, passing the barns, stables, and grain towers. Three industrial trailers edged the property before it gave way to the bull yards, and Kelly parked next to a row of dirty trucks, her little sedan a miniature vehicle among the bulky ranch equipment.

She glanced around as she walked through the packed-dirt parking lot, noticing that not much had changed. The clucking of chickens and the lowing of cattle met her ears, attributes that indicated this was indeed a working ranch. Kelly sidestepped a particularly large stone in the path. She'd have dust all the way to her knees by the time she made it inside. Everything about her spoke of a city businesswoman entering a whole new world, but she'd had to wear her heels. This was an *interview*.

Unfortunately, the metal steps and ramp were grated, creating a veritable gauntlet for her Jimmy Choo's. She supposed the heels, though fashionable and absolutely the perfect statement for this outfit, weren't exactly ranch attire.

She shifted her weight onto the balls of her feet and made it up four steps before her right heel sank through the metal. She set down her purse and tried to wrench the shoe free as she balanced on her toes. The Texas heat caused a trickle of sweat to form on her forehead. She did not want to enter the interview dusty, heelless, and now sticky.

She swung her hair over her shoulder, the movement throwing her off-balance. She gripped the railing to steady herself and prepared to make another attempt at freeing her shoe.

"You know, most ranch hands wear boots," a man said behind her.

Kelly's heart tripped as a strangled sound came out of her throat. She straightened, her hand smoothing down the back of her skirt, where a high slit was located. Had he seen anything?

She pressed her eyes closed. She'd never felt out of place on this ranch, and she wasn't going to start now. "Yes, I can see why," she agreed. "However, I didn't get the memo." Kelly opened her eyes and twisted to see who she'd need to avoid on the ranch. Because she was going to get this job, sweaty, mismatched, and dirty notwithstanding. She expected to see a cowboy—preferably one with a multi-purpose tool he could use to cut her free.

But this man, standing over six feet tall, didn't wear the regular stonewashed jeans and long-sleeved shirt. No siree. Not a boot or a belt buckle was in sight. Instead his pressed khakis and black polo accentuated his athletic body. Biceps strained against the sleeves of his shirt, a clear testament that ranching did a body good. Maybe he drank a gallon of milk everyday too. The only two indicators that he belonged in Texas were the cowboy hat perched naturally on his head and the panting dog at his side.

Kelly's reasons for wanting the position suddenly shifted to a completely new level. She gave herself a mental shake—she needed a job, not a boyfriend.

"Ma'am." He took off his hat and ran his fingers through his thick, brown hair. She couldn't tell from his sly smile and the amused sparkle in his eye if he was secretly laughing at her predicament or if he'd seen way more leg than she'd intended. She found herself returning his devilish smirk. Why was her stomach doing that floaty thing? She suppressed it and smoothed her hand over the back of her skirt again.

As he settled his hat back on his head, Kelly twisted and slid her feet out of the toes of her shoes. She turned around carefully so as to avoid touching the jagged metal, and placed her feet back on her shoes. Good thing she'd taken all those dance lessons. Still, her calf muscles hadn't been used this way for a long time.

As she took in his form again, she recognized his cobalt blue eyes still sparking with mischief, his straight, long nose, and his square jaw where that smile remained.

"Squire?" She wobbled a little as she spoke.

He seemed startled at the use of his name, his smile fading. Squire studied her for a moment, thunderclouds darkening his eyes into a shade of gray that reminded Kelly of the churning ocean. "I don't think we've met," he said.

Oh, they had. He just possessed a lot more to admire now than he had in high school, including a pair of unforgettable dimples that appeared as his grin returned. "Are you going to clue me in?" he asked. "Or just stare at me until your name appears in my mind?" He folded his arms across his broad chest and quirked his eyebrows.

She blinked rapidly, embarrassed that she'd been caught gawking. "I'm Kelly Russell." She shook her head, wishing she could shake away the words just as easily. "I mean Armstrong. Kelly Armstrong."

"Like, Bond. James Bond?" His throaty laugh tickled her ears. "Sorry. Doesn't ring a bell."

He shrugged like it was no big deal that he didn't remember her. Kelly couldn't understand how he could've forgotten. She'd practically lived down the hall in his sister's room.

"Yeah," she said, still balancing backward in her shoes, the heel still jammed into the metal steps. "Remember, I was on the cheer squad with Chelsea? I slept over here all the time?" She peered at him, but his face remained impassive, stoic.

"Chelsea had a lot of friends," he said. "Were you one of the gigglers?"

"No!" Kelly blew her hair out of her eyes, but it stuck to her forehead. She gave up hope of going into the interview without a bucket of sweat dripping from her face. "Remember how we used to choreograph dances and make you judge us?" Kelly emitted a nervous giggle before she could quell the sound.

"You just wanted to watch football, and we'd drag you into the back yard and make you watch us do our high kicks." She attempted the move now, realizing too late that her skirt was too tight for such things. Her foot barely made it above her knee and that slit allowed a blast of air to go up her skirt.

Squire's eyes closed briefly as she pressed down her clothes once more. The dog whined, somehow sensing her stupidity and warning her to *stop now!*

She'd lost her mind. *So this is what it feels like*, she thought. She'd let Squire completely undo her composure. Still, it bothered her that he didn't remember her. She took a deep breath, trying to refocus on the impending interview.

"Okay, well, whatever. Maybe you can help me get out of this mess." She pointed at her shoe and tried for a carefree chuckle. It sounded more like a strangled cat. At least it wasn't a giggle.

Squire joined her on the fourth step, steadying her as she turned around and stepped back into her shoes properly. "Why don't you just take off the shoe and then yank it out?" He released her and continued up the stairs while his dog slipped past them to lie in the shade. "In fact, I would've removed my shoes first, climbed the steps and then put them back on. At least shoes like that." He gave her a flirtatious wink, and her memory stumbled. Maybe this man wasn't Squire Ackerman. Kelly had certainly never seen him with more muscles in his body than stars in the sky. And he'd never flirted with her.

"I'd like to see you wear shoes like this," she muttered, her gaze murderous as she glared at him.

"I would *rock* shoes like that, darlin'," he said. "And Kelly? I remember your high kick being much...higher."

Her heart cartwheeled through her chest. He did know who she was! That little snake.

Before she could formulate an answer, he entered the building and let the door crash closed behind him.

"Take the shoe off, *darlin'*," she mimicked, but she did what Squire had suggested. The metal was just as hot and ragged as it looked. She balanced on the ball of her foot, trying to do as little damage as possible, this time to her skin. Her heel came free, and thankfully, it had only suffered a few minor scrapes.

"Is he always like that?" she asked his border collie, but he simply looked at her with a pleading expression, as if to say, *Please don't attempt that high kick again.* She vaguely recognized the animal, but she couldn't recall his name. She did remember that Squire had always loved his dogs. "Bet he'd help you if you got stuck."

She removed her other shoe and scampered up the rest of the steps barefoot. As she slipped back into her heels on the safety of the rubber mat outside the door, Kelly wiped her brow, sent a prayer heavenward that she could ace this interview, and took a deep breath. Then she pushed open the door.

―――――

SQUIRE ACKERMAN WINCED AT THE SOUND OF THE DOOR banging closed behind him, the metal on metal reminding him of being trapped in the tank. Immediately, the smell of hot gears and diesel fuel assaulted him, though the more accurate scent in the administration trailer would be men who worked with horses.

He took a moment to center himself, grateful he'd managed to navigate the stairs and enter the building without Kelly seeing his limp. As he strode down the aisle toward the ranch hands, he wasn't as successful. He'd been back at Three Rivers long enough for them to get used to his somewhat stunted gait, and they all busied themselves as they sensed his approaching fury.

"Where's Ethan?" he growled at Tom Lovell, the only cowboy who hadn't found a pretended task upon Squire's arrival.

"Sent him out to the north fence, Boss." Tom's gum snapped as he chewed it. "You said it had popped its rungs."

"How long's he been gone?"

"He left about seven." Tom stared steadily back at Squire, something the Army major appreciated. *Tom would make a good general controller*, Squire thought. But Clark sat at the front desk, and he'd run the operations on the ranch for almost as long as Squire had been alive.

Squire grunted his acceptance of Tom's answer and hurried around the short, semi-permanent partition. The shoulder-height wall separated the front area of the trailer, where the cowboys met and received their assignments, from the row of permanent offices he'd built into the back.

His father's door was the first on the left, Squire's second, and their accountant occupied the last office.

He might as well start thinking of it as Kelly's. Squire

knew his father had already hired her in his mind. The interview was simply a formality.

Squire's phone buzzed in his front pocket, but he waited until he'd made it inside his office, shut the door, and flipped the lock. Only then did he remove his phone, already knowing who had texted. Squire sighed, wishing he'd never taught his mother how to use technology.

Has Kelly arrived?

Like she didn't have her nose pressed against the front windows, watching and waiting for Kelly's car, simply so she could text him about it. She'd also sent message after message last night, each asking if Squire could handle seeing Kelly again. Her last one had said, *Forget about last time. This is your second chance.*

He'd ignored all her messages until that one. Then he'd sent back, *There was no last time, and there is no this time. Mom, stop!*

He definitely wanted there to be a *last* time. His invitation to her senior prom proved that. Her rejection screamed through him as loudly now as it had a decade ago. There would definitely *not* be a *this time*.

He leaned against the locked door and closed his eyes.

She hadn't driven the forty minutes to the ranch to find a new husband, he knew that for certain. He couldn't let the lines between them blur like they had last time.

At least he'd assigned Ethan a task in a remote quarter of the ranch. A calculated move, since Squire knew Ethan was the best looking cowboy employed at the ranch, with the biggest ego. He would've hit on Kelly before she even made it into his father's office. Squire had sent him away to protect her from Ethan—not because he was jealous or worried about the competition. Definitely not because of that.

Squire knew the moment Kelly entered the building, and not only from the way the walls vibrated as the door slammed shut. That sound would never become familiar, and Squire blinked away the blinding images of smoke rising from a mangled heap of metal that used to be a tank. The one driven by Lou.

Though dangerous, he focused on what he could remember about Kelly to help drive away the memories of his last deployment. The scent of her perfume had stuck with him through the years. As he'd passed her on the stairs, he'd caught the same whiff of cocoa butter and honeysuckle he'd always associated with her.

Kelly's voice floated through the thin walls of his office. "Thank you, Tom." Squire stuffed away the twinge of guilt that he'd caused her embarrassment. *He* hadn't worn impractical footwear to the ranch.

The walls shook again, Squire's signal that his dad had arrived. He'd expect Squire in the interview, though he'd already decided to hire Kelly. Squire didn't understand the point of the interview if he was going to hire the first person who walked through the door.

She's the only *person,* he reminded himself. Still, she'd barely made it *through* the door, what with those ridiculous shoes. He'd had to employ his military training to keep his face blank while he'd spoken to her.

Pretending he didn't know her may have been childish. Crossing his arms made him appear imposing and big, and he knew it. He'd done both on purpose to keep her at arm's length. He hated that she turned him to mush with a tropical scent and a smattering of freckles.

He took a cleansing breath, praying for the strength he lacked. He'd experienced plenty of frustrating situations during his dual deployments overseas. He could weather this too, especially since Kelly Armstrong had made her interest clear years ago. Nothing between them had changed. He was still Chelsea's little brother, someone Kelly had overlooked so often Squire had felt so completely invisible he'd sometimes startled when she spoke to him.

His phone buzzed again, but he chucked it on his desk before yanking open the door and heading toward his father's office, taking careful seconds to make sure his left leg didn't outpace his right.

Squire studied Kelly from a distance before he entered the room. Her turquoise blazer gave her a feminine figure, with a white blouse barely visible underneath. She wore those four-inch black heels and just the right amount of makeup to be professional. Her sandy hair fell halfway down her back; her light green eyes were as magnetic now as they'd been ten years ago.

He crossed his arms. A stampede of raging bulls did not scare Squire Ackerman. Bad weather could not deter him. Women did not affect him.

Major Squire Ackerman had complete control over himself, his emotions, and what he let other people see.

Especially Kelly.

"I am fearless," he heard her say as he stepped closer to

the doorway. "Who else would leave their cheating husband in California, trek halfway across the country with their four-year-old son, and attempt to start over?" She tried for a carefree chuckle, but her eyes caught his as he moved into the office. The sound stalled in her throat. She crossed her legs and gave him a pointed stare, but her gaze didn't flicker to his injured leg.

"Sorry I'm late." He settled on the corner of his dad's desk, ignoring Kelly completely though his fingers curled into fists, needing to corner and interrogate the man who'd cheated on her. "What did I miss?"

His father glanced up at Squire. "Miss Kelly said she can get Three Rivers back in the black."

Squire snorted. "How did *Miss Kelly* say she'd do that?" He reached down and opened a drawer in the desk. He pulled out a thick stack of file folders. "Because our last guy left us in a mess of trouble." He dropped the files, which were incomplete financial records, on the desk. They made a deafening bang.

Kelly flinched. She swallowed, a nervous movement that drew his attention to the slender column of her neck. Frustration frothed inside his chest, filling and fighting and overflowing until he felt choked with longing for a future that could never come to fruition. He wished he could go back in time and stop himself from asking her to the prom. Maybe then he'd have his dignity. Maybe then he could look her in the eye. Maybe then he'd be glad she'd applied for this job.

"I'd need to see the files in order to articulate a proper plan," she said, only a slight tremor in her voice.

His dad nudged the stack forward. "Take 'em."

Kelly eyed the paperwork, which probably weighed more than she did. She stood and dragged the folders toward the edge of the desk, staying a healthy distance from Squire. "I can come back tomorrow with a proposal."

"No need," his dad said, and Squire knew what was coming next. He stood up and put his hands in his pockets in an attempt to look bored.

Sure enough, his dad said, "You're our only applicant. If you think you can do this, the job is yours."

Kelly stared at him, unblinking.

A shiver squirreled down Squire's back at the same time his stomach clenched. "Dad, let's not be hasty." He glared at Kelly like she'd somehow bewitched his father into offering her the job. He knew she hadn't, just like he knew it was easier to act like a jerk to put distance between them. If she didn't like him, then she'd avoid him. The very thought made his heart tumble to his shoes, but he needed the distance.

He turned away from her and leaned closer to his father. "We can't afford another disaster."

"I won't let you down," she said.

Squire's blood squirmed in his veins at the assurance in her voice. He couldn't believe her. She'd let him down before and didn't even have the decency to admit it. He gave her another sweeping glare as his father clapped his shoulder.

"Show her to her office, son." He tipped his head her way. "Clark out front will give you the paperwork you need."

"Thank you." Kelly smiled and shook his father's hand, but he pulled her into a hug.

"It's good to see you back in Three Rivers, Miss Kelly."

Squire wished he didn't think so too. The fresh ink on her divorce papers felt like a shield he should wield.

"Thank you, Frank." She turned to Squire, almost like she would shake his hand too. He stepped back, a clear message for her to keep her handshakes to herself.

"This way." He led her down the hall, past his office, and into the last one in the back corner of the trailer. It was where he'd discovered the discrepancies between his father's bank accounts and the quarterly reports.

He'd never been so angry. So frustrated. So helpless. Not even when his tank platoon had been targeted in Kandahar and he'd lost four men in his company, been injured himself, and witnessed the more horrific things that fire did to human flesh. No, this betrayal ran deep, and it meant his parents couldn't afford to retire anytime soon.

Squire had never felt the love of ranching the way his father had, and his father's father before him. The ranch needed to stay in the family if his parents had any chance at surviving financially, which made it disappointing that Squire didn't have an older brother.

But he understood duty, always had. Even though he wanted a different life, somewhere else, if his dad wanted to retire, Squire would do whatever he could to make the transition easier.

Kelly flipped on the light and entered her office. She'd

lugged the files with her, and Squire considered taking them from her. *What could it hurt?*

But he knew what it would hurt. He'd worked too hard for too long to build those walls around his heart.

"Let me take those," he said anyway, his voice much softer now that he was alone with her. She had to stretch up while he bent down, his forearm cradling hers, as she transferred the load to him.

She stumbled, her shoulder crashing into his ribcage. A grunt escaped his mouth, and she gasped. "I'm sorry." She stepped back and tugged on the bottom of her jacket.

"It's fine." He moved to the desk, a definite limp in his step and a flush rising through his neck. He watched as she inspected the built-in filing cabinets, ran her finger along the blinds covering the single window, and tested out the chair behind her desk.

She finally looked at him. "I like it."

"Great," he said dryly. "It's not like we'd change it if you didn't."

She gave him a withering look. "Come on. It's me, *Kelly.*" She tried a smile, and he allowed himself to return it halfway.

He knew who she was. She was the girl who danced with his sister. Who slept over on the weekends. Who'd bewitched him so completely he'd convinced himself a senior would go to her prom with a sophomore. If she'd gone with someone else, he might've understood.

He shoved the sourness down his throat where it belonged.

While he hadn't been this close to Kelly in years, the

real prize she offered was solving the ranch's financial problems. He couldn't forget that.

He'd moved on with his life. So had she. She'd gone to college, gotten married, had a kid. And now a divorce.

He allowed himself to fully smile. Maybe she wasn't out of his league anymore. *She most definitely is*, he corrected himself as he stepped closer to where she sat. "You still know any of your dance moves? Besides that pathetic high kick, of course."

She threw her head back and laughed. "I'm sure I could choreograph something for you. Remember when I used to do that?"

"Yeah. You and Chelsea were so annoying."

"I'm sure we were." The glint in her eye spelled *mischievous*. "So do you make it a habit to leave helpless women trapped in your stairs?"

"You're hardly helpless, darlin'." Squire sat in the chair opposite of her desk with his arms crossed.

She busied herself with the files, shifting them around without really changing anything. "I also don't remember you being such a scoundrel." Though she'd moved away from Three Rivers, her Texas twang remained. He liked it, and wanted to hear her say his name in her pretty little voice.

"I don't remember you wearing such high heels," he shot back.

The silence lengthened between them, until Kelly asked, "How's your mother?"

She hadn't forgotten her Texas manners while she'd been gone. Squire would give her that. "She's good. She's given new definition to the word overbearing now that she knows how to text. But she's good."

Kelly leaned forward, and Squire caught a glimpse of her younger self, the girl he'd crushed on so long ago. "You don't like your mother texting you? Why? It cramps your style while you're out digging ditches?"

Squire could've sworn she was flirting with him, but the idea was ridiculous. She was coming off a messy divorce and had moved in with her parents. He'd heard what she'd said about moving halfway across the country alone. She wasn't looking for a relationship, especially with her new boss.

"As a matter of fact," he said. "It does. Digging ditches requires a lot of concentration. Texting is distracting."

"Don't dig and text." The flirtatious sound of her voice wormed its way straight into his heart. He'd remembered a lot about her, but her voice had faded quickly. He realized now how much he liked listening to her talk. "That is so you."

His pulse galloped, slowing to a trot as he leaned forward, like they might share something meaningful if they got just a little closer to each other.

Her phone chimed, and she jumped up. "That's my alarm. I need to get back." The playfulness and hope drained from her voice and face. She glanced up and smiled, but it had lost its savor. Squire watched the weight of real life descend on her, clouding the girl he'd once known.

"Can you help me get these to my car?" She indicated the folders.

"You don't need to look at them tonight," he said. "You start tomorrow. Look at them then."

She blinked a couple of times, confusion racing through those beautiful eyes. "I'll just take a couple folders." She picked them up and stepped toward the door just as Squire did.

Close enough to feel the gentle heat from her skin, Squire found a flicker of fear in her expression. He wanted to reach out and comfort her, ask her what her ex had done to her to make her so nervous, demand to know how he could have changed her into someone other than the Kelly she'd been.

Instead, he said, "You really don't need to take those. The ranch'll still need your help tomorrow." He moved into the hall ahead of her.

"Is it really that bad?" She joined him, her purse swinging between them.

"Just about." Squire noticed the silence in the front of the trailer. The cowhands had gone out on their assignments for the day, leaving Clark alone at the controller's desk.

"Miss Kelly," Clark said, heavy on the cowboy accent as he handed her a manila folder. "If you fill these out and bring 'em back tomorrow, I'll get y'all on the payroll."

Kelly grinned, tucked the folder into her purse along with the others, and thanked him. Clark barely acknowledged Squire, something he was used to. Clark knew everything about the ranch, from how to run it to how to let it run itself. If Squire was being honest, Clark should've taken over as foreman.

They both knew it, and it seemed like every other cowboy on the ranch did too. He had his work cut out for him to win over the staff and figure out how to manage something as vast as a cattle ranch. He'd tried some of the tactics he'd learned in the Army about taking over a company when the commander had been killed in action. But cowhands weren't soldiers, and they hadn't quite warmed to him the way his comrades in Afghanistan had. Squire had learned that men would trust him when he showed them they could.

He needed to do that at Three Rivers, but he hadn't quite figured out how.

Kelly didn't know any of his failures on the ranch, and she didn't need to. He wouldn't burden her with his unrealized dreams, permanent physical injuries, and financial troubles.

She removed her heels before stepping out of the admin building, and he had a momentary flash of him sweeping her off her feet and carrying her down the steps.

Longing lashed his internal organs like a whip. Thoughts like that were why he needed to put so much distance between them, why he needed to constantly remind himself of the duties he'd taken upon himself as ranch foreman. He had to find the missing money before he could even think about anything but the ranch.

"See you tomorrow."

Squire focused, the fantasy of him and Kelly dissolving as he realized she'd already made her way down the stairs and to her car. She waved, and he watched her climb into her sedan and drive down the road, kicking up dust as she went.

He frowned at himself, needing a cattle gate on his emotions to keep them contained. He glanced toward the stables, wondering how he could possibly endure day after day with Kelly so close.

SECOND CHANCE RANCH is available now!

Order it in ebook, paperback, or audiobook by scanning the QR code below.

THREE RIVERS RANCH ROMANCE SERIES

Escape to Three Rivers, Texas for small-town charm, sweet and sexy cowboys, and faith and family centered romance. You'll get second chance romance, friends to lovers. older brother's best friend, military romance, secret babies, and more! The Three Rivers cowboys and the women who rope their hearts are waiting for you, so start reading today!

Second Chance Ranch (Book 1): After his deployment, injured and discharged Major Squire Ackerman returns to Three Rivers Ranch, wanting to forgive Kelly for ignoring him a decade ago. He'd like to provide the stable life she needs, but with old wounds opening and a ranch on the brink of financial collapse, it will take patience and faith to make their second chance possible.

IVORY PEAKS FARM ROMANCE SERIES

Experience true Rocky Mountain life in the Ivory Peaks Romance series! You'll get more Hammond family romance, second chance romance, and all the heartwarming and uplifting family fiction you're craving. Ivory Peaks is the perfect escape for anyone looking to feel loved, cherished, and like they belong. You belong right here in Ivory Peaks!

His First Love (Book 1): She broke up with him a decade ago. He's back in town after finishing a degree at MIT, ready to start his job at the family company. Can Hunter and Molly find their way through their pasts to build a future together? Can his first love be the one that becomes forever?

SHILOH RIDGE RANCH IN THREE RIVERS ROMANCE SERIES

Meet the cowboy billionaires in the southern hills outside of Three Rivers! They love God, horses, the land, and family, and all 12 of them are looking for love in the small Texas town where they grew up. Start this Christian family saga romance series and spend time with people you'd be happy to call YOUR family too!

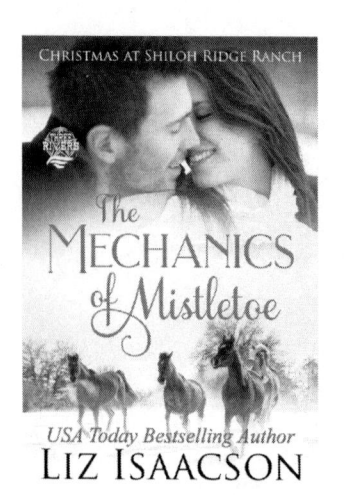

The Mechanics of Mistletoe (Book 1): He can be a teddy or a grizzly. She's a genius with a wrench. Can the pretty mechanic tame this cowboy's wild side, or will they both be left broken-hearted this Christmas?

ABOUT LIZ

Liz Isaacson writes inspirational romance, usually set in Texas, or Wyoming, or anywhere else horses and cowboys exist. She lives in Utah, where she writes full-time, takes her two dogs to the park everyday, and eats a lot of veggies while writing. Find her on her website at feelgoodfictionbooks.com

Made in United States
Cleveland, OH
27 October 2024